BEHIND
CLOSED DOORS

Stories of sanity, suffering and secrets
from Lockerbie Writers

Edited by Godfrey Newham,

Paula Gilfillan and Kerrie McKinnel

Contents

Illustration/Photograph Copyright Information

Dedications

In loving memory of my mother (Jean). – B.H.

For my husband Paul. Thanks for listening. – C.O.

To Mam and Dad for always being there, and Lockerbie Writers for making me feel so welcome. – D.R.

For my children, R & A, without whom I may have met every deadline on this book with *more* than an hour to spare! – K.M.

To my family, friends and Lockerbie Writers for their support. Love you all! – K.J.R.

To penguins everywhere – without you, I wouldn't have had a story. – P.N.

For William, John and Margarett:

>The battles that we seek
>
>be they great or small
>
>if we don't wear His armour
>
>we'll never win the war.
>
>- R.D.

Acknowledgements

By Kerrie McKinnel

Thank you to everyone who has supported the publication of this, the second anthology of short stories and poems from Lockerbie Writers.

Special thanks, in no particular order, go to: Godfrey Newham and Paula Gilfillan for their tireless editing; Vivien Jones for providing the introduction; staff at the Townhead Hotel and the King's Arms Hotel in Lockerbie for, respectively, providing a cosy and welcoming venue for the meetings of Lockerbie Writers and their sister group A Novel Approach; staff at Lockerbie and Annan Libraries for offering us a venue for the launch of this book; and to the Scottish Book Trust, who have provided us with funding in order to hold these launch events – and to print our first batch of anthologies, which will be gifted to members of the local community.

It goes without saying that this book could not have been created without the efforts of all members of Lockerbie Writers. This has been a mammoth effort and has been more than two years in the making, but we believe it has been worth every crossed-out word, each cup of tea gone cold while we debated the length of a sentence, and every single one of those million-and-one drafts.

Thank you once again to our family and friends for all the proofreading, hot drinks, and for listening to us complain!

Finally, an enormous thanks to you for picking up this book. We hope you enjoy reading it as much as we have enjoyed writing it!

Introduction

By Vivien Jones

"… The best words in the best order."[1]

It sounds a simple enough instruction but is always the result of hours of sharing peer and self-analysis of a piece of work. That the resulting work seems effortless is the magic of the process which the members of Lockerbie Writers have employed in *Behind Closed Doors*, their second anthology. The stories explore the inner lives, the deeper realities of a range of characters, in which the speakers tell their tales almost entirely without long descriptions of landscape and settings. We are invited to listen only to the essential.

What struck me first reading through the work was the wealth and breadth of vocabulary at work, obviously the result of time-consuming re-drafting, of paring work down to what must be said. Never more surprising than in a bare set of voices telling a family's history wholly through the emotions they feel (*Meia And Me*) or with the quirky humour of a penguin's life, carefully researched to keep it credible (*The Secretiest of Secrets*). There is spare rendering of family trauma (*Reboot Pending. Against All Odds*) often with a twist of the supernatural in the tail, sometimes told with a wicked humour (*Number 4, Parliament Street. Lady with Edelweiss*). There are tales that play with notions of time, guilt and sanity, sometimes both (*The Dalnessie Assignment. A Fond Kiss*) and many that explore the extraordinary interior lives of people who seem 'normal' on the surface *(The Missing Key)* but maybe quietly suffering.

I am a great believer in the value of writing groups. They are so often the medium through which people who have wistfully said, "I always wanted to write, but …" find the opportunity to get beyond the demands of work and family and face the challenge of

---

[1] Samuel Taylor Coleridge reportedly said these words on 12th July 1827. The words were noted and published by his nephew Henry Nelson Coleridge in the two-volume collection, *Specimens of the Table Talk of the Late Samuel Taylor Coleridge,* which is available from various publishers. For more information, visit: http://www.thisdayinquotes.com/2011/07/poetry-best-words-in-best-order.html?m=1

the blank writing pad with only a pen to work with. Plus, their imagination. Plus, the support of others. Of course they also sometimes serve a social function with the tea and biscuits and chat as welcome as the work but the writers here represented have moved beyond such simple ambition, responding to prompts that the group suggests to make and refine work that aims to say something valuable, more complex than mere description, more focused than anecdote. It is evident that the writers have paid close attention to plot development and on expanding vocabulary and these features have enhanced their writing.

I know too how much work goes into putting a manuscript together and that it is often overlooked, so I would like to express my appreciation of the care with which the book has been put together. I was pleased to be invited to write this introduction, even more once I had read the work with so many *best words in the best order.*

Well done to Lockerbie Writers.

Preface

By Steph Newham

Lockerbie Writers' Chairperson

Who really knows what goes on Behind Closed Doors?

As a group, we none of us realised where this idea would take us. Now with all the hard work, peer reviews, editing and re-writing behind us, we are faced with the answers. The months of speculation are over.

We are proud to present our answers to you, our readers.

Open the door
and step into each mind.
What insanity, suffering and secrets
will you find?

Reboot Pending …

By Deborah Redden

It's been 20 years since the accident. Twenty years, since a drunken ass saw fit to get into his car and mow my father down, as if he were nothing more than a blade of grass. What makes it worse is the fact that he got away with it! They never found him. Vanished, the police said. Car burnt to a crisp. Of course, Mum wouldn't accept it, still hasn't. She's always on the lookout for the 'fire-breathing demon' who took her husband away. I suppose it only stands to reason, really. If you'd lost the love of your life, and the person responsible for their death had never been found, wouldn't you go looking? Wouldn't a lead – a distinctive tattoo, or maybe a broken tooth – spur you on, making you walk the streets until your head hurt, and your feet were nothing but nubs?

Of course it would! It would drive anyone to search, and we did. We were a team. A mother-daughter powerhouse, looking for an unknown face. We travelled miles in that beat-up Escort, our noses assaulted by body odour and slowly-rotting food. Eating held no great importance for Mum; instead of stopping to enjoy a meal – like sane people would – we ate on the go, stuffing our faces at breakneck speed, disposing of scraps where we sat. And that was us, for the first six months at least. After that, things took a turn for me, and I found it hard to leave the house without sweating.

It was a strange phenomenon, me morphing into Miss Havisham as Mum became my Pip; my world, once a gem, now appearing so monstrous. But there was no stopping it. The panic grew, the noise was too much, and before we knew it, I was housebound.

I did feel guilty, leaving Mum to her own devices. But I was grateful for that patch of time we had together: that pause button that allowed us to bond through grief. If nothing else, playing detective meant I could live outside my head for a while, join the real world, function for an hour or two. Granted, trawling hospitals, bars and anywhere else you might find the perpetrator of a fatal hit and run, mightn't be the most advisable way for a child to spend their days. But I was eight. I was grieving, needed a distraction, and cartoons weren't cutting it.

Looking back, I suppose Mum was the same. I suppose she needed a task, something more than domestic duty and the neighbours' heartfelt sorrow to drag her from her bed. So, I don't blame her for those days on the road. In fact, I'm thankful. If she hadn't kept me busy, I'm not sure I'd still be here now. But I do wonder, sometimes, if it occurred to her how odd we must have looked; an unkept woman and her boogey-nosed urchin, scouring the streets day after day.

*

Still, that's all over now. All old news, mouldy old history that's of no interest to anyone but us. And I'd like to say we've got over it, that I've buffed myself off and furthered my life. But I can't. I'm still stuck in this room, filling this screen with guff, and living with a woman who resembles my mum but who's actually half zombie. She keeps me, you know. Pays for everything, works twelve-hour shifts just to keep us straight; nurse by night, Sherlock by day. It's sad, but part of me still expects her to pound on my door, and say, 'I found him, Robyn! I found him in a bar! The shit just confessed while pulling my pint!'

But hey, that's us, the exploited Beauty and the parasitic Beast! Mum's the former, of course! Speaking of which, it's ten o'clock. She'll be home shortly, a crumpled Brigitte Bardot, battered by the rigours of an eventful nightshift. I say this, because it's always eventful at Rosewood Care Home – haven for the infirm and elderly. There's always some argument or fracas to settle. Some frisky old streaker to report.

But have no fear, a gaggle of flustered damsels won't hamper Mum's exit. She'll be back. Rocking in as she always does, turning the key in the door and pounding our rickety stairs with those standard-issue clogs. She'll be tired, of course. She always is, after the graveyard shift. That's why I try to be upbeat, less of a loser and more of an optimist, shouting 'Hey!' as she passes my door.

It's her dressing table she'll be aiming for first. That tasteful little French number that reminds her of wealthier times. She's always loved that thing. Taken pride in its curves, the delicate ribbon of filigree that sweeps its shapely outline. This is where I learnt we were rich, that it was Great Granny's house we were living in, her money that lined our pockets. All years ago, of course, when I was innocent, and everything still had that pinkish hue.

I was six-ish at the time, sat in front of the mirror with Mum brushing my hair, and Dad at my feet struggling to buckle my shoe. Their voices were hushed, so I knew I should close my ears. But you know what kids are like – the faintest whiff of a secret and, well…

I'll never forget that day. The way Mum caved as she spoke of the family who'd disowned her, the ones who'd called Dad a commoner. Oddly, that look – that air of pained existence – isn't far from how she looks now. I've seen how she sits at that mirror, sweat offending her nostrils because she hasn't the energy to shower. How she still applies moisturiser, even though she's crying. The only difference is, I'm to blame now. There's no phantom family to take the hit. No gilded Granny to save the day, to take me by the shoulders and say, 'Okay, Princess, so the money's gone – devoured by your shrinks and your private tutors. But what's the plan? You can't stay cooped forever!'

Not that I'd have a notion what 'Queenie' would say; she was dead before I was born. But Mum was her favourite – Granny's little treasure – and I can't help thinking she'd be pissed. Angry because Mum's been lumped with me: 'the moping waster!' But I could deal with her imaginary disgust, the flashbacks, the nightmares, my guilt over ruining Mum's life. I could deal with it all, if it wasn't for our lovely neighbours.

You see, around these parts, I'm prime fare. 'Robyn Forrester Freakazoid' – a one-stop-shop for gossiping crones. Not surprising, I suppose. I am a bit odd: the girl who went into hiding, and never came out. But do they really need to go on about it? Do I really need to be the weirdo, the looper who couldn't cope with death, with the sight of her father's body plastered over the tarmac? It's not like I choose to live like this – like I suddenly went shopping one day and came back wearing agoraphobia and PTSD. They're illnesses, not fashion accessories!

Twits, the lot of them. As if I'd want to sit up here, in a room fit for the Adams family, with greasy hair and nothing but a laptop and hundreds of dog-eared books for company, when I could be outside, enjoying the first tweets of spring, jogging along with the in-crowd. I mean, look at this place: it's a shit heap. And I can't understand why anyone would think I'd stay here out of choice. Still, that's what you get, when you're a flat-broke loser living amongst the rich: playful derision and healthy disrespect.

Now, I know I'm hamming it up slightly, that I'm sour at my lot. But I'm not totally crazy, and I do know hatred when I see it. Take Desmond Crowe, for example.

He's always on his soap box; preaching to all who'll listen about the time he 'saved my life'. He went and collared a salesman last week – you know the sort, zit-faced and eager? Anyway, sales complete, Des saw his chance, using his pink-tint poodle to hamper the poor sap's exit.

'We found her in her nightwear!' he boomed, getting all handsy. 'Pyjamas on the High Street, can you imagine? The poor child was a laughing stock. Of course, as soon as I saw her, I knew there was something amiss. It's all in the glaze of the eye, you see … that fixed stare of the feral animal. So, I said to my wife, "Margery dearest, we must get this child home. Back to the safety of her mother. The poor woman must be distraught." And she was, you know. But I suppose I'd be loopy too, if my child were a nutcase frightened of a wailing kettle. She'd scaled her bedroom wall, apparently – held on tight and … whoosh!'

Whoosh! I'll give him WHOOSH! He's lucky I didn't turn feral and take a leak from my bedroom window, right over his lovely waxed dome. The only thing that stopped me was his nonplussed audience. The salesman looked horrified! Not surprising, really. I mean, he was barely 19; his legs weren't built for that amorous dog!

Still, it'll all be at an end soon. No more snippy neighbours, or endless days of nothingness for me. You see, a makeover's in progress. Myself and this shit-heap room are getting our act together, turning all sharp and organised. Oh, it'll take time, I know it will; a hoarder's crap won't be cleared in a day. But I'll get there eventually, even if I need to work nights, or howl at an ominous moon.

Hurray, I hear you shout! The girl has found her mojo, gone and got her shit together. But why? Why, after years of hiding away, of shirking from the smallest excursion, jumping at the slightest noise, is she suddenly waking up and considering leaving her hiding hole? Well, I'll tell you why, the answer is very simple: the hounds are circling, and I've decided to do something about it.

It all started months back, with Mum bursting into my room, her nurse's whites dishevelled. I was about to express my concern, suggest she go to bed, maybe a little nightcap, when I noticed the set of her eyes. They were furious: as sharp as an apple, and just as round. She was shaking.

'Can't you pick yourself up a bit, Robyn?' she gasped. 'God knows, I love you. I love you more than I do myself. But if I hear one more word from that smug, self-righteous Crowe, I won't be responsible for my actions! Have you been spying on them, Robyn? Well, have you? According to her, you've been using the binoculars again … so, where have you hidden them this time? Well?'

I was devastated. Mum looked repulsed, stood in my doorway, as if us getting any closer might make her heave. But I told the truth. I had to – the evidence lay under my pillow, a traitorous lens glinting in the sun.

'Of course I've been spying on them!' I said, nerves making me giddy. 'How else do I keep a check on things, keep an eye to how Mr Crowe and his awful wife have been treating you? I've seen Margery, Mum … The way she glares at you like you're dog shit. And she might seem "all innocence" flopping over that fence of hers, all boobs and sympathy, but she's no angel. "One is simply concerned for your safety," my arse. All that woman is concerned over is her image and the way we're pulling it down. Mum, she's a battle axe in Gucci!'

'Oh, come on, Robyn!' replied Mum, suddenly finding her voice again, and gripping my wrist with a force fit to break it. 'Cut me some slack. I'm not totally brain dead. I've seen and heard what they're like, and yes, I'll give you this: they can be a bit abrasive, uppity even, but I refuse to believe they'd spread rumours just to see us gone!'

I laughed so much that I started to shake. Tears welled up in my eyes. I mean, really, was she honestly that naïve? There wasn't a day that went by without them spewing some sort of tripe about us. And now here it was, working – driving a wedge between us.

But I shouldn't have laughed. Mild hysteria or not, it was never going to wash. Not with this blistering ball of rage hurtling its way towards me.

'DEAR GOD, ROBYN!' – I was stunned – 'You've a nerve, talking about people when you're up to worse yourself! You're standing there laughing as if it's all a big joke, and everyone's here for your amusement. We're not, you know! Some of us want a life! Some of us want more than small-time tittle-tattle and four manky walls for company. In fact, for some of us, it would be enough to leave the house, safe in the knowledge that nothing dodgy's going to happen. But then again, we don't all have daughters like you, do we Robyn? You're a nightmare. I've given up my life, spent all that money. And what for, eh? You're still not right, and you couldn't give a stuff about me. Not. One. STINKING. STUFF!'

*

And that's why I'm sitting here now, hoarding a pile of skeletons. I couldn't let Mum think I didn't love her, that I'm all take and couldn't give a monkey's! So I've been collecting the bones. Granted, it took a while – getting my hand in, getting to know the groove. But once I got going, I was surprised at how easy it was, turning from innocent snoop into world-class hacker. Did you know that you can access a computer's camera in seconds, see accounts at the touch of a button, or turn a mobile into a microphone? No, I didn't either! Not until I went looking. I've had my eyes opened. If cyber terrorism has taught me anything, it's that you need to be cagey with your details.

It was Des who popped up first: Des T. Crowe, Proprietor and CEO of Tuscan Tastes ltd. Now this was no great surprise. Des is always harping on about his juicy little vineyard in Italy; nice little money spinner, apparently. But what he failed to mention – to me, my mum or his WIFE – was the fact he has another family there. OMG! I mean, jackpot! I couldn't believe my eyes, the randy old sod, syphoning all his money to his 'Gina Lollobrigida' when Margie wasn't looking. And as for his Mediterranean sprogs! Well, all I can say is wow, poor Margery. Not that she's much better, with her acidic tongue and her ill-advised hate mail.

So there, now you know! Now you can see how desperate I am. How badly I need to make things right. Oh, if only I could let fly – collect everything I've got and shove it in their sanctimonious faces. Of course, I've thought of it more than once. One touch of a button, and it would all be there, waiting in their inboxes, shining like a beacon in a foggy night sky.

But I can't. I REALLY CAN'T! Something's telling me not to – appealing to my decent half, willing me not to indulge in blackmail. Maybe it's Queenie, the saviour of the underdog, or possibly even my dad, I don't know. But whatever it is, it's driving me nuts. My head's cracking into shards; sanity's nearly impossible.

But, here's the thing. I've never done this before. I mean, how long do I wait? What's the protocol for forced apologies that may never come? It's been a week since I sent the email – 'I KNOW YOUR SECRETS, PIPSQUEAK! BE NICE OR ELSE!' – but there's been nothing. Nothing but silence. The Crowes have gone quiet. Left me in limbo, waiting for the 'ping' of my inbox.

It hasn't all been bad, this pause of normal procedure. It's made me realise that I don't want to live this way. That I need to move quick, do something before I'm seventy; so far, I've done nothing with my life. And there's one thing I know for certain now, I need to look out for Mum more. Treat her with respect, think less about me and more about us. So, I've started to look at ways to make money on my own steam, something other than cold-hearted bribery. A blogger, or something with graphic design, anything that would help me build my confidence, before I re-join the rat race.

Still, that's all ifs, buts and maybes. For now, I'll have to make do. I'll clear up this shit heap, wash my greaseball hair, and dream of better days. Days where I'll be earning; have a nice little poke with which to spoil my mum. I may even put this house right: restore the parquet flooring, and those grand chandeliers looming in the bowels of the loft. Maybe we'll go to the Ritz, because Dad had always dreamt of that and never got the chance. Or jump on the train! Roll on down to the seaside. Spend the day in the sun, eating chips from newspaper, reminiscing over happy times. And once we're finished – once our fingers are licked clean and our bodies are weary from the fullness of the day – she'll turn to me and say, 'Do you remember him, Robyn? How he'd make sandcastles just up the beach there? How he'd spend hours getting it perfect, togs pegged at the waist, just for a dog to foul it or the waves to gobble it whole! Do you remember?'

And I'll have to admit that I do remember, because I dream of it every night, willing it to be here and now. So I'll look at her then, beaming in the glow of new beginnings, and say, 'Yes Mum, yes I do. Will we go see him, up at the grave? It's been a while, and we could even bring flowers for Queenie …'

A Fond Kiss

By Frank MacGregor

In 1962, the village of Sandemans Reach was a row of flint and brick cottages on the main road between Oxford and Didcot. Around the village green there was a small grocery shop with a dilapidated awning, a post office and the Red Lion Inn. The picturesque cottages were built to house workers on the local estate; now they were occupied by affluent professionals from nearby Oxford. Opposite the village green was the 14th century flint and sandstone church of St Bartolph. Abutting the church – hidden in the foliage of large-leafed lime trees – was the entrance to a lane. At the foot of this lane was a substantial red-brick house. In the house, Arthur Sinclair stood before the library windows, and watched as the evening shadows devoured what remained of the day. A weary sigh fled from his lips as he stretched, ran his hands through his greying hair, and turned from the window.

His nightly measure of whisky, two fingers, wouldn't suffice; not tonight. He poured until the dark-golden liquid filled the glass. Sinclair gulped a mouthful, but he didn't swallow; he held it in his mouth, swilled it around, savoured the wild peaty flavour, then let it trickle down his throat. Easing his lean body into his battered old leather club chair, he stretched his long legs before him, closed his eyes, and let the comforting warmth of the whisky course through his body.

Sinclair couldn't have foreseen the repercussions that accepting the invitation would bring:

'You are invited by the Master to join him as his honoured guest at the annual alumni dinner.'

Earlier that year, at the age of fifty-seven and after twenty-eight years of unstinting service to the law, Sinclair had, at last, achieved his life's ambition: Her Majesty the Queen had seen fit to appoint him a Justice of the Supreme Court of the United Kingdom. The invitation from the College had come a couple of months later. Sinclair had an intense dislike of formal gatherings. He avoided them like the plague. He was useless at small talk, and ill at ease in large social gatherings. This was different, he'd convinced himself; he was invited by the Master of his old College in honour of his achievement. But thinking back, he knew why he'd accepted, though it shamed him to admit it – he'd sought the approbation of the alumni.

On the night, the night of the dinner, Sinclair recalled his relief when he arrived and saw the friendly face – and now ample figure – of his old pal from College days, Percy Oldstein. They'd both gone to Oxford on scholarships: Percy from a school in the south west of England, and he from Scotland. They'd both studied law. Whatever the reason, right from the start they were friends. Now Percy was Professor of Jurisprudence at their old College. Not until they neared the end of the meal, did Percy speak of Oliver.

'I must confess I was surprised when the Master told me you had accepted his invitation,' he'd said. 'You have never liked formal affairs, have you? Anyway, I'm glad you came. It's given me the perfect opportunity to ask a favour of you. Would you consider acting as mentor to a particularly gifted law student?'

Mentoring was a long-established College custom, a custom Sinclair always managed to sidestep. He was about to roll out his excuses when Percy waylaid him.

'Before you say no, and I can tell by your face that you want to, let me make my case,' Percy had prattled on. 'I have never met anyone with as quick a grasp of law as you, Arthur, that is until I met Swinbourne. I am sure, in return for mentoring, he could be persuaded to accept a quid pro quo of some sort; perhaps he could re-catalogue your library. I know you would be the perfect mentor. I should tell you that Swinbourne is at Oxford on a scholarship. He is here, at the dinner. Would I be imposing too greatly on our friendship to ask that you, at the least, talk to the lad?'

How could he have refused?

Percy made the introductions and left them. Sinclair remembered how impressed he had been by his first sight of Oliver. He was young, tall, and had the firm body of an athlete. And he was undoubtedly handsome. At first, their conversation was everyday, stilted. Oliver said he was from Sheffield, and was the only son of his widowed mother. He seemed reticent, shy. But it all changed when their conversation turned to matters of law. The transformation in Oliver's personality was striking; his shyness and diffidence vanished. Oliver was animated, and his face was luminous with enthusiasm. As they talked, it became clear that Oliver was, as Percy had said, a bright young man – and that was why, at the end of the evening, Sinclair suggested, 'Why not come to my home at the end of Lent term? We can have a proper discussion and you can have a look at my library. Let's see if we can work something out that is agreeable to us both.' And that was that, or so he'd thought.

The conversation had all but vanished from Sinclair's head when, sometime later, a letter arrived from Oliver. The letter referred to their conversation at the dinner, and asked if the offer still stood. Sinclair recalled his mixed feelings on reading it; premonition, sixth sense, call it what you will, but he'd felt a strong urge to ignore the letter. The more he considered it, the more he was convinced that he couldn't spare his time. There was a particularly complicated case coming before him, a case that would take all his resources; Sinclair didn't need a young law student hanging around. But he hadn't acted on the urge; instead, he'd scribbled a brief note saying the offer stood.

Sinclair's memory of the day, the day Oliver first came to his home, was as vivid in his mind as if it had happened yesterday.

'The day is too good to waste sitting indoors,' he'd said. 'Why don't we go for a walk? We can talk as we walk, and if we are of a mind to, we could call in at the Red Lion and have a drink.'

At the end of that wonderful day – when Oliver was about to leave – Sinclair had heard himself say, 'Since the Easter sittings don't commence until the end of April, why not come and stay here? I have plenty of room. It would be so much more convenient than travelling back and forth, and it will give us a greater opportunity to discuss your studies; and perhaps you can help me with the reorganising of my library.' Sinclair had given no prior thought to the idea; it had come right out of the blue. By the stunned expression that appeared on Oliver's face when Sinclair proposed it, it was obvious he'd been taken aback by the suggestion. For a few moments they'd stared at each other, both unsure of what to say, then Oliver's face had lit up and he'd laughed.

'I would love to take up your kind offer,' he'd said.

Sinclair had chosen to live a quiet and ordered life; it suited his temperament and, until now, he had felt no need to change it. When he was at home, there was routine. He would breakfast at seven thirty: two three-minute boiled eggs with tea and white toast. At midday he would have a light lunch; his evening meal was at seven, after which he would read until he retired for the night. Oliver changed that. Over the time he stayed with him Sinclair learned: that Oliver preferred coffee to tea; that he preferred brown toast to white; that he liked his eggs poached rather than boiled; that he was an early riser; and that he preferred to shower rather than bathe. It was all trivial, familiar, and comfortable stuff. They talked, they laughed, and Sinclair was, to his surprise, completely at ease with their growing familiarity. Until last night. Last night, Oliver had kissed him.

When it happened, Sinclair was shocked, embarrassed, but most of all, confused.

'Christ almighty, why did you do that?' he'd shouted.

'I don't know,' Oliver had answered, 'I just –'

'You just what, for Christ's sake? You don't just kiss another man,' he'd said.

'I'm sorry, I thought you wanted me to kiss you …'

'Why should you think that?" he'd blustered. Sinclair could not deny he liked the young man, but what was it he felt for him? Was it affection, the affection an older man has for a younger man of promise; did he see in Oliver something of his younger self? 'I am tired, Oliver, I am going to bed,' he'd said, 'we'll talk of this in the morning.'

Sinclair's mother had often asked him, 'Why don't you have a girlfriend?' She may have suspected and feared his inclinations? But if so, she never spoke of it. Unlike friends at school and university, he'd felt no great need of female company. He'd often wondered why. Long ago it had suited Sinclair to believe that he was asexual. It was a comfortable explanation. He would have been content to meet his Maker believing that it was so. Last night, in his naivety, Oliver had asked a question of him. Oliver had asked, and Sinclair had panicked.

When Sinclair was appointed to the Bench, he had unashamedly basked in the aura of inviolability that surrounded it; an unassailable wall of probity and conformity. If he were to continue an association with Oliver, he would breach that wall. Sinclair's love of the law was no passing affair to be jettisoned when it became inconvenient; it was a lifetime's passion. It would be easy to rationalise that a small breach in the wall would have little effect on the structure. But a breach, however small, could lead to a weakening of the foundations. Could he, a Justice of the Supreme Court of the land, knowingly commit an overt act of vandalism?

Staring into the dark depths of his whisky, Sinclair toyed with a fanciful notion: if the gods of fate offered him the opportunity to turn the clock back, to expunge Oliver from his life, what would he do? Would he grab the offer? Earlier, as he was browsing through his library, he had come across an Oscar Wilde quote. He couldn't remember it word for word, but it read something like: *there are times when you can choose either to live your own life to the full or to drag out some false existence just to conform.* Wilde's reluctance to conform had led him to prison and ruin. Sinclair was not so naïve as to believe that a relationship with Oliver, if it had continued, could forever have remained unnoticed and unremarked. The law establishment was akin to a small provincial town; scandal, or the merest whiff of it, spread like the most virulent of plagues.

Rising from his chair, Sinclair crossed to the windows and closed the curtains. What would happen, he wondered, if he continued his association with Oliver? What would be the repercussions for Sinclair? There were others on the Bench, though it was never talked of, who he suspected had a similar inclination. If he maintained discretion in his relationship, then it was likely a blind eye would be turned. Was that what he wanted? Here he sat, sipping his whisky, wrapped up in his own concerns, but what of Oliver, he thought. What would be the repercussions for him if they continued the relationship? No protective wall of inviolability surrounded him. The archaic law of the land dictated that reports of homosexual relationships must be investigated; should the least whisper of unnatural behaviour attach itself to Oliver, all hopes which Oliver may have harboured of advancement in the law would disappear.

Sinclair had always enjoyed these end-of-day moments. The house was quiet, apart from the intermittent sound of sputtering rain on the windows, and the low moan of wind through the eaves. But it was not so tonight; tonight, he was restless. Oliver had thrown a stone into the calm waters of his existence; he had created ripples, and a part of him resented the intrusion. Another part – a less hidebound part – was half-ways tempted to let things run their course. There was something exhilarating about the prospect. Having someone to confide in, someone to share his thoughts with, to do the things that having a partner allowed; it was tempting. But Sinclair knew this was silly and impractical. There comes a time, a time when even the most ardent of dreamers must come face to face with who and what they are, as Sinclair had done, or so he'd thought.

This morning they'd sat together, after breakfast, and attempted to talk of the kiss. But Sinclair's mouth had become strangely out of sync with his brain; he'd muttered and mumbled incomprehensible rubbish. Both had avoided the questions to which they wanted answers. It was easier to be vague and not to confront what had happened between them; to leave unsaid what they both knew; to accept it had been an aberration, of no significance, and to agree it would be best, for them both, that they never see each other again. It was all very civil, very matter of fact. This morning Oliver left.

Today, thought Sinclair, had been an absolute shit of a day. Now his glass was empty. He didn't usually drink this much, but tonight he felt a need; Sinclair poured until his glass was three quarters full. That would do, he thought, he wouldn't be able to get out of his chair if he took any more. All day, since Oliver had gone, Sinclair's mood had veered between depression and half-boiled self-righteousness. He'd wandered around the rattling silence of the house like a demented soul. He'd done the right thing, hadn't he? If he was so sure he had, why in hell's name was he so miserable? He'd tried to keep himself busy, but questions kept repeating and repeating in his head. Could they have continued as friends? Why had he asked Oliver to his home, and why had he asked him to stay? How many times had he sat on the Bench and been amazed at the ability of people to deny the truth? To hear them lie so convincingly that they had come to believe that what they said was true. Was that what he, Sinclair, was doing? *Are we all self-deceivers?* Sinclair wondered.

Enough was enough, Sinclair thought. He was tired, and the whisky had dulled his senses. Nothing would be gained by constantly churning over what had happened, and besides, what was done was done; life would go on. Gently lifting himself from his chair, Sinclair swallowed what remained of the whisky, and made his way upstairs. His breath was stale; it was disgusting. He had drunk too much; he would have to clean his teeth before he went to bed. Looking into the bathroom mirror, Sinclair was taken aback by the haggard face that looked back at him.

'Sinclair, you're a bloody mess,' he muttered aloud. 'Why are you crying?'

The Secretiest of Secrets

By Paula Nicolson

Once upon a time, in a very cold place called Antarctica, lived a young penguin called Pupillo who loved to swim, chase fish and go for walks. Pretty much what all penguins like to do, heh? However, Pupillo had a secret, and because he thought it was the secretiest of all secrets, it made him feel very sad. Now, you may be asking what the secret was. If I told you now, then it wouldn't be a secret, would it? You'll just have to read on and find out!

Pupillo lived with his mum, dad and nan in a house made of pebbles (penguins call them rookeries). Every day his mum would go to the sea and hunt for fish, his dad would collect pebbles to make the rookery bigger and his nan knitted jumpers for poorly penguin chicks. One day, Pupillo asked if he could go for a swim with his mum.

'Sorry Pupillo, not today,' she replied, slinging her netted fishing bag over her shoulder.

'But Mum, you know I like swimming and I would stay with you all the time!'

'Oh Pupillo, I've promised to swim with the other penguin mums today so we can catch lots of fish and krill for the rookery for the old-age penguins, and I'm late already! I need to get down to the sea quickly.'

Pupillo looked down at his small bumpy feet; they didn't carry him anywhere quickly.

'Maybe tomorrow?' she said.

Pupillo looked up at his mum. 'OK!'

'Thank you, sweetheart,' his mum said as she stroked his beak. She slid out of their front arch and waddled away.

Seeing Pupillo looking sad, his nan said, 'Come over here and let's have a big Nan–Puppi cuggle.' She gave him a hug so tight against her soft, white feathery tummy that it took his breath away.

'Tomorrow eh? When Mum's not rushed off her feet.'

'I know,' mumbled Pupillo into his nan's tummy.

'You could help me collect more pebbles, son,' said Pupillo's dad. 'I think the new neighbours across from us have been pinching them. If it's not them, then it's some other penguins. This thieving never stops!'

Pupillo did not like collecting pebbles. He loved sliding on his tummy across the ice and chasing fish in the cold waters of the Antarctic ocean.

'Errum … Mum told me to tidy away my ice blocks,' said Pupillo. He waddled quickly into his bedroom before his dad had time to reply.

But what Pupillo did next would change his life forever.

While his dad was out searching for new pebbles and his nan was looking for a lost ball of wool, Pupillo crept out of the back arch.

'I can make it to the sea myself this time!' he muttered, and started waddling. 'I like walking. I'm going to get to the sea, go swimming and bring back loads of fish for tea!'

And a lot of walking Pupillo did. He walked and walked AND WALKED.

But Pupillo couldn't understand why he had to climb over lots of really big dry rocks. This land didn't look the same as when he walked to the sea with his mum! It was also very quiet; he could not hear the sea lapping the ice cliffs nor the daily penguin chatter. He was feeling hot and thirsty too.

'Oh dear,' he cried, 'I think I'm lost!' and with that Pupillo started to sob; big salty tears that ran all the way down his tummy to his tiny feet.

To make matters worse, a skua bird was circling above him. His nan had warned him about skuas; they often stole eggs from the rookeries. But then Pupillo spotted a cave!

He waddled as fast as he could to the cave and squeezed himself through its slit of an opening. He could hear his heart pounding and feel his hot breath on his flippers. He closed his eyes.

'I'll just wait in here for a bit, and I'm sure Mum and Dad will soon be along to find me,' he said to himself, but after a long time no one came. Pupillo peered out from the cave, but he was met with a sharp peck on his head and heard a loud voice.

'What are you doing out here, little penguin? You're a long way from home. Do you know where you are?'

Pupillo was too scared to speak at first, but eventually he plucked up the courage to use his 'big voice', as his mum called it.

'My name is Pupillo. Who's talking to me?'

'Well, you should've guessed by now. You saw me earlier and then you ran away from me,' chuckled the voice.

'If you're that skua, this isn't funny!' said Pupillo.

'Yes, I am THAT skua and I agree. A penguin, miles away from his family and being followed by a skua, is no laughing matter.'

'Where am I?'

'The Hidden Desert,' replied the skua.

'Oh no! I just want to go home!'

'You're not the first penguin to end up here. Every year, a few of your lot seem to waddle in the opposite direction to the sea and end up in this desert, never to return home!'

'Oh dear!' cried Pupillo.

'Personally, I don't want to see that happen to another penguin. The name's Sami. Fortunately for you, I don't find penguins tasty; I prefer fish. They're much easier on the stomach and don't make me burp. I'll show you the way back home and then I'm going to give your parents a good talking to. Come on out, kiddo.'

Pupillo crawled out of the cave and slowly walked over to the skua. Sami said he would fly above Pupillo to get a better view of the land ahead and, at the same time, shadow him from the sun and show him the way home. Pupillo had no choice but to put his trust in Sami if he was to make it back to his rookery. He didn't know why he believed and trusted this bird, but he had a feeling that he was telling the truth.

It took a long time for Pupillo to get back to his rookery; he arrived back to see a very frightened mum waiting for him at the back arch.

'It's OK! It's OK!' shouted Pupillo.

Pupillo's mum rushed forward and grabbed him tightly by his flipper, dragging him as quickly as she could into their rookery. Out of breath, Pupillo explained to his scared family how he had got lost and that a skua called Sami had helped him to find his way back home. Pupillo's family looked at each other, and then his mum went outside and saw that Sami was still there, cleaning his wing feathers.

'Err … excuse me Mr Skua? Thank you for bringing our son home without, you know, eating him.'

Sami coughed. 'Well, I was just glad I could help. The name's Sami, by the way. Did you know your son has no sense of direction?'

'Well … yes. All the other penguins his age seem to know their way to the sea, but he keeps getting lost when he goes on his own. He can't even tell his left flipper from his right! We just don't know why he's like this! We're worried the other penguins will tease him – or worse, he might not come back home one day – but we're just too busy to help him at the moment.'

'Mmm,' replied Sami.

'Pupillo knows he has trouble finding his way to places, but that doesn't stop him from trying to go for a walk on his own. He must've sneaked out of the rookery this morning without us knowing.'

'If you don't keep an eye on him, then next time he might not come back!' Sami said as he started to hop away, but then slowly turned towards Pupillo's mum and said, 'Let me know if I can help. He's only young and, as I told him, I don't eat penguins; not good for my tummy.'

Pupillo's mum paused. She had heard of penguins going missing before, but a skua helping a penguin? That was unheard of. Yet, he'd brought her son back home, alive! They had run out of good ideas on how to help Pupillo, and she knew he was sad staying at the rookery all day. Skuas never seemed to get lost, and as they could fly above the rock and ice, they always had a good view of the land.

'I may regret what I'm about to say to you, Sami, but I'm willing to strike a deal with you. Our summer is a really busy time for us grown-up penguins. If you'll be Pupillo's bodyguard and help teach him to find his way to the sea and back home again, we'll reward you with two fish a day.'

'OK, it's a deal! I'll be back first thing tomorrow morning,' and with that, Sami flew off.

Pupillo's mum returned to her rookery and that evening told the rest of the family about the deal she had struck with Sami. They all agreed that it was probably a good idea, for now. But Pupillo was not to tell anyone that he kept getting lost and that Sami was helping him. Pupillo felt sad; he liked Sami and he didn't like keeping secrets. After dinner, he went straight to bed because he felt very tired. Pupillo's mum, dad and nan stayed up and talked long into the night.

The next morning, Pupillo's mum left early to go fishing again. His dad had to stay and guard the rookery to stop the other penguins from stealing his pebbles.

'Puppi,' said his nan, 'your dad has found a pair of his old sunglasses for you to wear. He thinks that they will stop the sun from blinding you and then you'll see where you're going more easily.'

'Yuk! They're bright orange! The other penguins will make fun of me!'

'Do you want to go to the sea or not?'

Pupillo nodded, but then felt a waft of cool air on his back. It was Sami landing next to him. 'Nice glasses kiddo,' Sami said and winked.

Despite Pupillo's gripe about the sunglasses, they set off on their first journey together. Sami flew above and shouted directions down to Pupillo. But Pupillo still felt really silly wearing the sunglasses and couldn't see clearly where he was going either.

About halfway to the sea, Sami became distracted by a shiny pebble and lost sight of Pupillo. 'Oh crumbs! Where's he gone?'

Sami flew around for a while until he spotted the orange sunglasses lying near the door of an old hut the human explorers had built. Landing by the door, he could hear a knocking sound from inside. Looking in, he saw Pupillo wandering around in the dark, bumping into some old boxes.

'Pupillo!' he called. 'Come out of there!'

'Oh Sami. I'm lost again! I took the sunglasses off as they were hurting my beak.'

'OK, let's go home. This idea isn't working.'

With Sami's help, Pupillo made his way back home and told his dad and nan what had happened.

That night, the family talked again about how to help Pupillo, but no one came up with any new ideas. Later on, his nan was busy knitting. She noticed that her favourite ball of wool wasn't on her lap; following its woollen thread, she found the ball behind a pile of pebbles.

'I know!' she shouted. 'One of us could unravel a ball of wool as Puppi walks to the sea, and then on his way home, he would just follow the same woollen thread home!'

Everyone agreed that this was the best idea yet.

The next morning, Pupillo's mum tucked a big red ball of wool under her flipper and placed one end of the woollen thread under a very heavy rock near to their rookery. As she walked, she slowly unravelled the ball of wool, leaving a trail of red thread behind her. Pupillo followed, holding onto the woollen thread as he waddled.

Their path to the sea wasn't easy. They had to find their way around large boulders, and the woollen thread often got caught on the rocks. They then had to slide across an ice field. When they reached the ice cliffs, they put the last of the woollen thread under a big ice ball.

Pupillo and his mum went swimming and caught loads of fish. As Pupillo jumped out of the sea onto the ice, he was met by Sami, ready to help guide him home. However, Sami had been followed by a very angry penguin.

'Go away skua! Leave that youngster alone!' said the angry penguin.

'It's OK, he's here to help me!' said Pupillo.

'Help you? He'll steal your mum's eggs as soon as her back is turned!'

The angry penguin stood between Pupillo and Sami.

'Look mate, I'm just here to help Pupillo get home, nothing more.'

At this point, Pupillo's mum appeared and while she told the angry penguin that Pupillo was not going to come to any harm, she secretly nodded to Sami and Pupillo to start heading back home.

Pupillo picked up the red woollen thread from under the ice ball and waddled off quickly, gathering it in his flipper as he walked along. Sami flew off in a different direction, pretending he wasn't with Pupillo.

As Pupillo reached the boulders, a strong gust of Antarctic wind pushed him over and then rolled him over AND OVER the thread. He quickly became tangled up in it. His flippers were held so tightly to his body by the thread, he couldn't move at all!

'Help Sami! Help!' cried Pupillo.

Sami, hearing Pupillo's cries, dived down. He snipped at the tight woollen thread around Pupillo's body, using his beak like a sharp pair of scissors. Pupillo was now free of wool, but felt very bruised.

Sami decided he would hop along with Pupillo the rest of the way home rather than fly above, just in case the wind blew him over again. That night, the family all went to bed feeling sad.

During the night, Pupillo's nan had a dream from her chickhood. In the dream, human explorers visited the island. They were wearing thick woollen scarves around their necks in all different colours; some were stripy.

She awoke with a start and, leaping out of bed, she set to knitting a scarf for Pupillo as quietly as she could so she wouldn't wake anyone. By the time everyone had woken, she had finished it.

The scarf was brown, but at one end it had a lemon-coloured stripe and on the other, a red stripe. She put it around Pupillo's neck and crossed it over his chest, fastening it at his neck with a big purple button. The lemon-coloured stripe sat on the left side of his chest and the red stripe sat on his right side of his chest (looking down from Pupillo's beak to his feet).

As Pupillo looked a little puzzled, his nan told him how to use the scarf.

'Right, Puppi, put your listening ears on! Wear this scarf all the time. Use the lemon-coloured end to help you remember which is your left flipper. Can you hear that "lemon" and "left" both start with the letter L?'

Pupillo smiled.

'Use the red end to help you remember which is your right flipper. Can you hear that "red" and "right" both start with the letter R?'

Pupillo nodded.

'Then, use your left and right flippers to help you remember when to turn left or right along the path to the sea!'

'Oh, I get it now! Lemon for left, red for right! Thanks Nan!' said Pupillo, giving his nan an even bigger Nan–Puppi hug.

'Don't worry, Sami will still be looking out for you!' and she gave Pupillo a kiss on his head.

Pupillo left his rookery and saw Sami waiting for him. He explained what the colours of his new scarf meant. 'That's brilliant, kiddo! I might need one for myself in the future!' Sami replied, and winked.

That morning, rather than fly above him, Sami hopped alongside Pupillo. They began to talk.

'So kiddo, to help me find my way back to my nest, I look out for "markers". They tell me where I am and which way to turn; you know, a boulder, a funny looking rookery or a big icicle.'

Pupillo nodded.

'OK, as we hop and waddle to the sea, we're going to look for markers, and then when we have to turn left or right, we can use your scarf to help you remember which way to turn.'

Pupillo nodded again. He had to put his trust in his nan's scarf and Sami.

The first marker they chose was their neighbours' rookery, which had a square roof.

'When we reach the square roofed rookery, we turn right. So, which is your right flipper?'

Pupillo looked down at his scarf. 'This one,' he said, waving his right flipper in the air.

'Great kiddo!'

'I know that because the red end lies this side of my tummy, so that means it's next to my right flipper!'

'You're catching on fast, kiddo!'

Pupillo jumped into the air and waggled both his flippers in excitement. 'Let's see what we can find as the next marker, Sami!'

Pupillo and Sami hopped and waddled on together. The next marker they came across was a tall penguin-shaped boulder.

'At this boulder that you say looks like your dad,' said Sami, trying not to laugh, 'you need to turn left and then follow the narrow rocky path down to the ice field.'

'OK, I know that this is my left flipper,' said Pupillo waving his left flipper, 'because the lemon end lies the other side of my tummy, which means it's next to my left flipper!'

'Correct! Let's turn left and follow the path to the ice field.'

It wasn't long before they reached the ice field. Sami and Pupillo slid across its smooth surface on their tummies and used their feet to push themselves along; this was a lot faster than hopping and waddling and it was much more fun! It was a simple straight path across the ice field, and they were going so fast and laughing so much when they arrived at the sea, that they nearly fell off the ice cliff! But they were just in time to join Pupillo's mum for her last fish hunt of the day.

After Pupillo had finished swimming, he jumped out of the sea and onto the ice. Sami was waiting for him. As they hopped and waddled back to the rookery, Sami again helped Pupillo remember the markers they had chosen on their way to the sea (and when to turn left or right).

When they reached Pupillo's rookery, they both jumped up and down with excitement! Pupillo's dad and nan came out and joined in with the jumping.

'I did it! I did it! I walked the whole way to the sea and back without getting lost AND I even remembered which was my left and right flippers!' shouted Pupillo. 'Thank you Sami!'

'You did all the hard work, kiddo.'

As Sami turned to leave, Pupillo's mum arrived back home and stopped him.

'Thank you, Sami,' she said. 'Now that you've taught Pupillo the way, I don't think he'll need your help again. He should be able to do it himself.'

She gave him six fish, but he wouldn't take them.

'Pupillo deserves the fish instead.' But Pupillo started to cry.

'What's the matter Puppi?' asked his nan.

Turning to Sami, Pupillo said, 'Sami, I'll miss you so much. Can you to walk with me to the sea every day, please?'

Sami looked at Pupillo's mum, dad and nan. They all nodded at him and smiled.

'OK kiddo. Lucky for you, I like hopping and chatting to penguins!'

From then on, every morning, Pupillo would wear his scarf and waddle and chat with his mum all the way to the sea, showing her his markers and when to turn left and right. Sami would meet Pupillo at the ice after his swim, and hop all the way back home with him.

Over time, Pupillo got to know the other penguins in his colony and plucked up the courage to tell them his secretiest secret. He also told them how Sami had saved his life and how he used his special scarf to help him to tell his left from his right flipper. To his surprise, a few of the penguins said that they knew other penguins who often got lost. They said they would help Pupillo if they ever saw him wandering the wrong way and wondered if his nan could knit more scarves; this would really help the penguins that had the same problem.

As the months passed, Pupillo's sense of direction got better and better. But he always wore the scarf as an anchor to remind him of his left and his right; just like the advice of a good friend. Speaking of which, Sami and Pupillo remained friends for the rest of their lives and the other penguins learned to trust Sami too. But the greatest thing Pupillo learned was this: that if it could help make his life and the lives of other penguins better, the secretiest of secrets was better shared.

*

Pupillo is based on the true life of the Adélie penguins who live on the Antarctic continent and its neighbouring islands. After watching a BBC documentary about them, I learned that Norwegian scientists had observed that a few Adélie penguins walked not to the sea, but inland where they died in a barren rocky valley of an Antarctic 'desert'. At first, they thought that this behaviour was due to sun blindness, but further research revealed that some Adélie penguins suffer a brain malfunction which causes them to lose their sense of direction; it's as if they don't know their left from their right. I thought this fact had parallels to disabilities within our own human society ... and my story was born. Other facts, such as stealing pebbles from each other's rookeries and that Adélies are the feistiest penguins on the planet, are also true. Sami as a helpful skua is completely made up I'm afraid, but wouldn't it be nice if skuas and penguins got along?

In common with other Antarctic animals, the Adélie penguin population is being affected by the ongoing impact of human activities locally and globally. If you would like to know more about Adélie penguins, please visit:

https://www.wwf.org.uk/wildlife/adelie-penguins

The Missing Key

By Betsy Henderson

Janet woke with a start and looked at Alan, who was breathing noisily, struggling to stay alive. She had tossed and turned most of the night, worrying about her husband and what would happen. Every day he was worse than the day before, and every day she tried to be brave. But she knew she was kidding herself. She didn't know how much longer she could live like this, waiting, praying, hoping but knowing there could only be one outcome. Dreading the day, but longing for it at the same time.

'Are you there, love?' he gasped. 'Can you get me a drink?'

She struggled out of bed into the freezing bedroom, cumbersome, feeling like a pregnant hippo. She wished this baby would hurry up and arrive. It was already ten days late and every day seemed like a year. Please, please, please let it be born soon, she begged. Please let it be born while Alan is still here. Please Lord, do this one thing for him, let him see his daughter. For some reason, she knew the unborn child inside her would be a girl. She just knew – or maybe that too was wishful thinking, like everything else.

She grabbed her outsize housecoat from the hanger and swung it round her, before unlocking the front door, and filling up a jug from the outside tap. They had always meant to get proper sanitation in the cottage but since Alan had been invalided from the Army after the war, they had never had enough money. Life in their small Scottish town was hard but Janet hadn't cared as long as they were together.

She closed the door and filled a glass for Alan, before taking it back through to the bedroom. His breathing was becoming more laboured and his eyes vacant as if he was leaving her.

'Janet, darling,' he gasped, before lapsing into a semicoma. Janet rushed over to take his hand.

'Do you want me to get the doctor?' she whispered, although she knew it would be pointless. The doctor had already warned her the end would be sudden and there was nothing he could do. She gently touched her husband's face and briefly kissed his lips as she sensed him slipping away.

Alan gave a loud rattle, before taking his last breath.

'Oh, God no,' she gasped, 'I didn't mean this quick.'

She looked at his handsome face, now calm and serene, a look of contentment she hadn't seen for a long time. He could almost be quietly sleeping, she tried to pretend, but deep down she knew the truth.

She sobbed her heart out, not knowing whether to be happy or sad. At least he was at peace now, but she had no idea how she could live without him. She felt her baby move as if it knew what had happened.

'I don't know how I'll cope without your daddy,' she wailed. 'Please help me.' All their dreams had evaporated – all because of a stupid war neither of them had asked for.

She lay beside him, pretending he was still alive, feeling the heat from his body and wishing she could stay there forever. She heard him talking to her, telling her it would be all right and that he would still look out for her, that he would help her during the long lonely months ahead.

Eventually she got up and went next door to see her in-laws to tell them the bad news. Although they had been expecting it, they were still beside themselves, but Grandad took charge and she was able to relax a bit.

'You need to take care of yourself now,' her mother-in-law declared. 'The baby will need you more than ever.' They came back into the house with her and sent for the doctor to confirm the death.

Everyone was falling over themselves to be nice to her, but Janet wanted to scream. Nothing made sense any more. What was the point of her still being here? Why had Alan been taken, and she had been left alone? Was there a God and if there was, what was he playing at? All these questions went through her head. She couldn't make sense of anything and the more she thought about it, the more distraught she felt. The doctor tried to calm her, talking to her gently, telling her she must look after herself, she must keep healthy for the sake of the baby. The baby, the baby, the baby, she screamed. Everyone kept going on about the baby. What about her? What about Alan? She cried and cried for hours until eventually, tired and broken, she fell asleep.

That night, she kept waking up every few minutes and when exhaustion took over she dropped off again. She was falling into a deep ravine and Alan was floating above, trying to catch her, telling her to hold on. He called out to her; he would save her. She kept trying to grab his hand, but every time she got near, it moved just out of reach. She awoke to the sound of her own screams, the sweat clinging to her. Her worried in-laws were there, trying to calm her down.

At the funeral, Janet thought she was going to pass out; she had insisted on going to the cemetery, although everyone advised against it.

'He's my husband. I have more right to be there than anyone else.'

'Women don't go to the graveside,' her dad declared, 'especially when they're nine months pregnant.' But whatever anyone said, she didn't care. She was pleased to see the many friends and neighbours who had attended. She would do this one last thing for the man she adored, even if it killed her.

And it nearly did. Her daughter was born the next day. It was a difficult birth, lasting nearly 12 hours. But it was worth it: a beautiful fair-haired, blue-eyed cherub, whom she called Alana, because she was Alan's double; a constant memory, as if she needed one. Alana's grandparents spoiled her and gave her everything they could. Janet struggled for money, even though her in-laws helped her to buy coal and the odd thing from the corner shop. Because she was too young for the full widow's pension, she was only getting ten shillings a week, and that didn't go far, especially when she had to pay five shillings for rent. She knew she would have to get a job, but where and how – especially with a young child to look after?

The opportunity arrived when she heard of a young couple, Tom and Edna Carruthers, who had nowhere to stay. Apparently, they had lodged with Edna's parents, but there had been words between them, and Tom had been asked to leave. Janet didn't know the whole story, but assumed that Edna was a loyal wife and had left with him. Janet felt sorry for them, and needed the money, so she decided to offer them a home. She gave them the only bedroom in the house and she slept in the cupboard bed in the living room with the baby. They gave her five shillings a week and this paid her rent, allowing her to buy more food for herself and milk for the baby.

Things went quite well for the first few months, although Janet couldn't go to bed until Tom and Edna turned in and was often so tired, she could hardly keep her eyes open. However, the money just about made up for the inconvenience and she told herself it wasn't for ever. To be honest, she was half afraid of Tom. He was very abrupt and difficult to get on with and Edna seemed on edge most of the time. He started going to the pub two or three nights a week and when he returned, she could see he was drunk. On these occasions, Edna seemed very nervous and it was hard to hold a conversation with her. She would hide away in her bedroom and Janet often heard her crying. If Janet asked what was wrong, Edna fobbed her off with an excuse.

Janet suspected that Tom was knocking his wife about, but she couldn't prove it. She often heard banging and slapping noises coming from the bedroom. There would be muffled cries and shouts, but she could never make out what was being said. Janet found it very difficult to relax. Sometimes the angry voices woke Alana and it was difficult to coax her back to sleep.

One night, Janet heard loud sobbing and not being able to keep quiet any longer, she knocked on the bedroom door.

'What do you want?' Tom growled.

'Is there anything I can do?' Janet whispered, afraid to make the situation worse.

'Mind your own business,' he retorted. 'It's nothing to do with you.'

She crept away, unsure what to do, but knowing she had to resolve the situation somehow. She went back to bed but spent a sleepless night worrying. She knew she would have to do something; things couldn't continue the way they were. Even if she had been on her own, she would have been afraid, but she was terrified he would do something to Alana, something she wouldn't be able to prevent.

The following morning, the couple got up and acted as if nothing had happened, although Edna seemed more anxious than usual. Her hair, which she usually tied up in a ponytail, was brushed forward over her face and she was wearing more make-up than usual. Although the sun was shining, and the day already beginning to heat up, she was wearing trousers and a long-sleeved cardigan. It was obvious to Janet that Edna was trying to hide something, but before anything could be said, husband and wife hurried out the door and down the street.

Janet was left anxious and frustrated. She worried all day, knowing that something would have to be done to sort things out, but she didn't know what.

For a few weeks all was quiet. Perhaps things were settling, Janet hoped, and she wouldn't have to make any difficult decisions, but she knew she was only putting off the inevitable. Still, as long as it stayed peaceful, she could put up with it, if only for the money.

Tom worked at the market and sometimes, if there was an auction, he had to go into work early. On one of these mornings, Edna was late coming through from the bedroom; she should have been at work ages ago. Eventually, unable to put it off any longer, Janet knocked at her bedroom door.

'Are you OK?' she shouted. 'Aren't you going to work?'

A few minutes later, Edna limped out, holding onto the door for balance. Janet could hardly believe what she saw. She gasped in amazement as she looked at Edna's bloody head and the massive bruise covering the whole of one side of her face. She could hardly walk as she struggled through to the living room; her leg was obviously very painful and her left eye was almost closed. Janet could see the fear in her other eye, she looked desperate though trying to hide it.

'What's happened?' she gasped. 'What has he done to you?'

'Nothing, nothing!' Edna cried. 'I fell out of bed.'

'Don't be stupid!' Janet retorted. 'Do you think I was born yesterday? I know he's beaten you up and not for the first time!'

Edna shuffled over to the couch and collapsed. She tried to avoid making eye contact, but Janet sat down beside her and confronted her.

'You can't put up with this any longer. He'll end up killing you.'

'No, he won't,' Edna replied. 'It's because he loves me, he can't help it.'

'Of course he can. That's just an excuse. Do you really want to spend the rest of your life being scared to say or do the wrong thing? Do you want to be scared to go out, scared to speak to anyone, in case you do something that offends him?'

Edna just sat there and looked blank. It was as if she didn't care what happened to her. She had just given up! Janet was becoming more and more frustrated. She was trying to save the life of this woman who didn't seem bothered whether she lived or died.

Eventually Janet sighed in exasperation. 'You'd better go back to bed. I'll get some ointment for your injuries and make you a cup of tea. Perhaps you'll see sense when you've had a rest.'

The day passed in a blur. Janet busied herself looking after Alana and worrying. She didn't know what to do for the best. She sympathised with Edna, but she couldn't have a vicious brute like Tom in the house where there was a poor defenceless baby. God knows what he could do if he was roused. Her head seemed to be going around in circles, with nothing decided.

About three o'clock Edna got up, minutes before Tom got in from his shift. She'd had a wash and a change of clothes, and looked better. Tom strutted into the house as if nothing had happened. He looked at his wife, and Janet thought she saw a trace of shame on his face, but then within minutes he was making light of the situation.

'You made a right job of it when you fell out of bed,' he joked. 'You should maybe see a doctor.'

Janet was flabbergasted! She was afraid to say anything in case she made the situation worse for her friend, but she couldn't just ignore it.

'I don't think that's what happened,' she said. 'It looks like someone has had a go at her.'

Tom looked shocked. He was obviously not used to people arguing with him and he didn't know how to deal with it. His face clouded over, his voice became a growl and he glared at her menacingly.

'I saw her fall out of bed,' he snarled. 'Are you calling me a liar?'

'I wouldn't dare,' Janet replied, sarcastically. She looked at Edna with a mixture of sympathy and anger. 'Are you going to put up with this monster for the rest of your life? Come with me now and you'll be rid of him for ever.'

Edna looked scared. Janet knew she wanted to follow her but didn't have the courage.

Tom grabbed a poker from the fireplace and threw it at Janet, missing her by inches. He grabbed Edna and roughly pulled her towards him.

'You want to stay with me, don't you?' he smirked.

'Of course I do. I love you. Why would I want to leave you?' Edna retorted.

There was nothing Janet could do. She couldn't stay in the same house as this vicious monster any longer. She would be afraid to close her eyes, not knowing what he was capable of.

'Well Edna, if you come to your senses, there's always a home here for you.'

She grabbed Alana and wrapped her in a blanket, before rushing outside and banging on her in-laws' front door. On her way out, she shouted to Tom, 'I'll be back in an hour. If you're still here, I'll be calling the police to get you arrested.'

She waited an hour and a half before venturing back into her own house. She had left Alana with her mother-in-law, but her father-in-law went on ahead to make sure the coast was clear. The house was empty. Tom and Edna had gone. Janet started shaking. She knew she had done the right thing, but she was frightened for Edna. Janet knew it was up to Edna what she did, but Tom seemed to have some sort of hold over her. If only she would come to her senses. Janet felt frustrated and anxious, but at the same time angry that she couldn't do anything to help.

For a few days, all was quiet. Janet had no idea where her lodgers had gone, but she was afraid. A house key was missing and she was sure one of them had it. No problem if it was Edna; she would be able to get in if there was an emergency. But what if Tom had it? She had no idea what he might do if provoked. Janet spent many sleepless nights battling with her anxiety. Every sound she heard, she feared his return, and she was constantly tired from lack of sleep.

A few weeks later, she had just turned in for the night when she heard a loud rattling at the door.

'Who is it?' she cried. 'What do you want?'

'It's me, Edna. Please let me in.'

Edna was standing on the doorstep in her nightie, looking furtively around, trembling with fear. 'He says he's going to kill me, just because I said hello to my mother's neighbour.'

'Come in, quickly, before he gets here.'

They sat up most of the night, afraid to go to bed in case Tom tried to get in. Edna confirmed he had kept a key, so Janet's fears were real. The only remedy was to have the lock changed but they couldn't get that done until morning.

At least one good thing had happened: Edna had eventually realised that things were never going to improve. The only way she would find peace would be to leave her husband. She cried and fretted, kept saying 'What if?' but she knew she was only kidding herself.

'I'll go and see a solicitor tomorrow,' she promised. 'Will you come with me, for moral support?'

'Of course I will, it's time you got rid of that waste of space,' Janet replied.

The next day, Janet and Edna went into town. Janet arranged to have the lock changed. It cost most of the money she had left, but it would be worth it for her peace of mind. Edna made an appointment to see a solicitor the following week.

Janet hoped Edna would stay. If Edna was living with her, she would have a bit more money and hopefully things would start to improve. She would also be a help with Alana, and Janet might be able to get herself a part-time job.

But that was a long way off, she told herself. First things first.

Life settled down. For a few weeks everything was calm. Tom seemed to have disappeared and Edna was able to relax and get back to work. The two women got on very well without the threat of violence hanging over them, but Janet was always afraid it wouldn't last. She was sure Edna's husband wouldn't give up without a fight.

Her fears were realised within the month. night, just as they were preparing for bed, they heard a key being tried in the front door lock.

'It's Tom!' Edna whispered; terror written all over her face.

'Don't panic,' Janet replied, 'he can't get in.'

'I know she's in there,' shouted Tom. 'Let me in or I'll break the door down.' When no one answered, he became more violent, rattling the door and trying to put his fist through the glass. Luckily it refused to break.

The two women were afraid to move in case he heard them, but knew that if the baby woke, Tom would know they were there.

'I'll have to go with him,' Edna quivered. 'I can't risk him hurting you and Alana.'

Janet didn't know what to do. Her mothering instinct told her she had to protect her baby but, if Edna went with her brute of a husband, who knows what could happen? She was still wavering when they heard another voice at the window.

'Are you OK, Mrs Thomson? Do you want any help?'

Janet almost fainted with relief. She recognised the voice of Matt Crossley, who lived a few doors along.

'No, we're not,' she screamed. 'Is Edna's husband still there? He's trying to break in. Please help us!'

She ran to the door and gingerly opened it a few inches. She was just in time to see Matt throw a single punch at Tom, who fell to the ground, splaying across the pavement.

'He was trying to break the door down,' Janet shrieked. 'He used to be my lodger, but I put him out because he was beating up his wife. He's been trying to get her back, but she doesn't want to go. Thank you very much. You don't know how grateful I am.'

'No problem,' Matt smiled. 'It was a pleasure. I've heard a lot about him – none of it good.'

At this point, Edna appeared, shaking like a leaf. 'Thank you, thank you, thank you,' she gasped. 'I don't know how I'll ever repay you.'

Tom was starting to come round, a bit less sure of himself than before. 'I could get you done for assault!' he shouted at Matt. 'You could have killed me!'

'Just try!' came the response. Matt grabbed at Tom's lapels, forcing him to stagger backwards. 'If I hear another word from you, the police will be finding out all about the beatings you gave your wife. Oh, and by the way, didn't I hear something about sheep carcasses going missing from the market? *You* don't know anything about that, do you?'

Tom knew when he was beat. He slouched off into the night like the coward he was.

Janet invited Matt in for a cup of tea and a piece of her homemade bannock, and at last Janet and Edna were able to relax.

Edna was shaking, the events of the night catching up with her. She looked at Matt. 'I don't know how I can ever thank you,' she gasped. 'I might begin to get a normal life now.'

He gave a sly grin and looked questioningly at Janet. 'I can think of something.' He glanced back at Edna. 'You could always babysit, if Mrs Thomson will be good enough to come to the pictures with me.'

Janet laughed, 'Maybe it's time I started to live again too – and the name's Janet.'

For the first time in a long while, she was looking forward to the future.

Meia and Me

By Rita Dalgliesh

KIZZY

What goes on behind closed doors? Unresolved issues V settling scores.
A prissy miss, I was myself, didn't cross the line till Melvin came along.
Who'd believe when our baby was born she'd turn out creating a storm.
Meia full grown; can't handle what's going on, her dad and I divorcing.

A lonely child in foreign lands; born into the barracks of army camps.
Mum as warm as a deep freeze; Dad, a constant confidentiality.
When Melvin looked at me twice, I leapt at the chance of a better life.
My parents objected, my future they'd asserted. I'm a selfish daughter.

I don't know how I caught Melvin's eye; me being quite plain and shy.
Melvin's persistent; I maybe his first virgin. The reputation that follows
these warriors with uniforms, all muscles of masculinity and discipline.
Melvin goes AWOL. Trouble is, a glitch: he's sleeping in my bed not his.

Melvin and I have many discussions, get to know each other, it's intimate.
Explaining how his duties come about, the missions we can't talk about.
A crap shot to crack shot, zero to hero. Training; aiming for forces elite.
Emotions; manoeuvres in Ulster's unrest to the rest. Angola, Afghanistan?

Reminiscing; our situation, we didn't use contraception, what a cock up.
Expectations: future relations with a child, we're expecting. Melvin said,
'Marry me Kizzy.' Raymond's a comrade he'll witness. I trust implicitly,
A shotgun wedding, a military family; for the forces, seems appropriate.

I'm a scholar and outcast not embracing social life, a boring bookworm.
Growing up would have been great if Dad hadn't been absent or too late.
Missing from meaningful things I did; personal achievements, presentations,
graduation. Both parents renege; my marriage to Melvin, Meia's beginning.

Forget my father; his devoted wife. I took to swotting, not living.
I'm a first-class legal adviser; my mum retreated even further.
A privileged situation's sacrificed as Meia takes pride of place in life.
History repeats itself; my soldier joins his regiment, add secret objective.

Melvin left in the night; security a priority for soldiers' safety, my insecurity.
I wouldn't be like Mum. When my man comes home, we'll have some fun.
Miscarriages take their toll; our sex life hits a wall. I end up like Mum after all.
No point-four kids for us. Melvin deserves more; our relationship turns sour.

Then came the day Raymond, Melvin's best mate got blown away. At length my
husband can't comprehend for shock, shrapnel and trauma, the loss of a friend.
Returning from death's duty; waking in intensive care needing full-time nurture.
Orla, his proficient nurse reciprocates fervour. I see in their eyes; sparks fly.

The turning point in Melvin's welfare is already by his side, my visits now are
taking a slide. I'm a voluntary observer of future happiness I could never deliver.
That's when Meia goes off the rails; all grown-up, no pigtails. She met a crowd of
insatiable mates; they'd drop their kegs to get a kick. Feelings I'd long rejected.

Our beautiful daughter, a woman of the world, despises my lack of insight.
A degree I'd love to see her achieve. Her dad has a new love now you see.
Meia's fury knows no bounds; you can cut the atmosphere, here's a knife.
Behind closed doors I couldn't believe the stunts she pulled; lies she sold.

I'm asking Mum to take us in; humbling, make reconciliation, I've no option.
Meet the grandaughter you neglected. We left our mutual home for Melvin.
Living with Mum helps funds as financially embarrassed I am; just this once.
Deceitful as Meia is, my mum's never to suspect we're often at loggerheads.

But, Meia excels, bawls, shouts. Mum's ultimatum, cool it or clear out. We're out.
Almost demented living on Meia's terms 'tis a sad do, but to herself she stays true.
Pending settlements; Aiden's my mum's financial adviser, resolving overdue issues.
There's a job vacancy in his firm. Together we hit it off, find a home, doors open.

I'm ready to take a chance, a bit of romance. Meia has her eye on him; Aiden
shoots her down. The trouble this caused, nobody knows but Meia and me.
I gave up her dad too easily; he's history and that bloody Orla is so beastly.
We all want the same for Meia, settle down; find peace, a place in uni. Please.

Orla's a new reason for Meia's wayward living; if she wants to see her dad
she'll have to get through Orla first. They've been an item from the start.
If it was just flirting with her dad, could Meia handle it? Orla in my opinion
has a deep, dark sadness that vanishes when Melvin needs her inspiration.

Given a new start myself, I find my heart toward them melts. It won't be easy
going over old ground. If Orla can help Meia and stay sane, I won't stand in her
way; Melvin feels the same way. We parley for a day or two, break the ice.
Meia has a choice; we have a voice. Her future's in the hands of a psychologist.

Discretion: the better part of discussion. Meia is vexed, volatile and venomous.
Venting disapproval on us; threats of non-compliance. We prove our unity as
Meia looks at two options: see Orla and end up at uni or go your own way with
our blessing, bending rules. It's your future you're sacrificing. But Meia's no fool.

Aiden's started a new regime; we're in our own home, this wipes all slates clean.
Meia V Orla, time for change. Finally a computer whiz kid piques Meia's interest.
Meeting matches as she studies in university at last; this tamed our Meia's farce.
After all those men, found she preferred female partners full of satisfactory intent ... AND?

Meia calmed down when all was revealed. Who would have thought it all a shield?
I marry Aiden against all the odds. We're intellectually and physically sound; why not?
Meia and me experienced a lot; now our doors open to life's unexpected moments.
Happy days they may follow; for now we are invited to Orla and Melvin's wedding.

*

MELVIN

Knowing I wasn't the same as the rest; the DNA was put to the test,
experiencing a desire to join up, childhood leaves me desperate to fight.
Foster parents try to suppress what came naturally for me to express.
I meet Kizzy and the tables turn; I'm head over heels in love with this one.

I'm no saint, I've got goals; determination to leave this loveless hell hole.
Life's troublesome; nobody knows what goes on behind closed doors.
For foster fees in front of authorities; major and minor corruption's hidden
dutifully surfacing as they leave, scared when the door closes on me.

As Mrs Fucked Up has a go at me, slapping and shagging for all she's worth,
'You keep your mouth shut Melvin.' Says a nowt for that's what this scum
is all about wanting release for what's in its pants. I'm not up for shagging
the fucking bastard thing. Authorities won't listen; the brutality's not missing.

Mr Pissed-On-The-Proceeds says, 'Stay tight lipped.'; there's abuse, beatings.
A belt never far from my backside, I'm too young for these mixed-up feelings.
Education's wasted on me. I want to learn but there's no help for me see.
Money's all that mattered; put a life down the pan for free labour and sex.

Leaving the system as soon as I'm able, I join up; start to feel stable.

Discipline's easy, initiation's fun, a breeze; result, Raymond's a pal.

Going through hell and high water: a squad of recruits practise to shoot.

On leave we prowl around for the women that cost a few shillings.

Singles are dispensable; cost's not excessive, killed on the front line.

When I met Kizzy in her state, the Army could wait; I went that away.

AWOL I went once or twice; sleeping with Kizzy was a bit of alright.

Antics costing me well-earned stripes. It's on the front I'll have to fight.

Debating life into the night, not without fault as secrets I divulge,

pillow talk. Kizzy's pregnant. 'Marry me, make a first-class family.'

There was moaning and groaning but I made the grade; she stayed.

I got a ring; done the right thing, Meia's born. Our regiment deployed.

As time passes – and it's all we've got; I miss Meia growing up a lot.

Duty calls; we do our stuff, familiar with the game, terrain rough, tough.

There's undetected land mines underfoot, Raymond and I are blown up.

Staggered at my pal's demise, I'm motionless, speechless, cold as ice.

Army hospitals are in full use returning from death's duty. 'First-class treatment

for you then. I'm Orla, your nurse.' A woman of intellect. Lovestruck, I relent.

We grow close thanks to a daily diagnose of psychology; who knows what?

Need for progress increases. Kizzy realises, releases; happiness increases.

Meia is improbable; her nature strays, becomes impossible. I'm a painstaking

target: my daughter's on the rampage. Orla's anxious intervention's peripheral.

I've handled trouble, strife; been in the firing line at home and fields of battle.

My precious girl's grown-up, someone to be reckoned with; like me in my youth.

Kizzy's amenable, for my welfare and health she cares; just not upfront personal.
Lost babes; our relationship froze with rebuff. I get the property; money's fleeting.
Meia's visits I could do without, her attitude sucks. Orla orders her out of hospital.
At home a university offer, Meia has a place; a degree in the making if agreeing.

A dose of independence has proven useful; Meia could give lessons to my bloody
foster parents, but I grew up in the school of hard knocks and wouldn't grass.
Meia may have her mother's looks; she has my DNA for being in all bad books.
A madam she turned out, like the women Raymond and I paid; who can I blame?

Orla gave the insight; Kizzy gave her parental right and I was grateful alright.
Meia reaps the benefit of Orla's years in perseverance; caring for undesirables.
Orla's affection infected jealousy into Meia; an awful affliction, she had it bad.
We had to admit we hardly knew each other; not entirely our fault, duty called.

Recalling this little beauty, the times I closed the door, unaware of what I left behind.
I'd hear Kizzy say to Meia, 'Just like my daddy, yours too has to go far away to fight.'
Yes! Meia turned out to be a force to be reckoned with; what happens behind closed
doors is not always revealed – until the damage passes. Issues never resolved for fear.

The Army: released pent-up issues only I could decipher, benefiting many missions.
Resolutions for us humans, falling in love; cope with it, it's full of short-term unions.
Meia's not afraid of new experiences or ungovernable tempers. Lads get the heave.
Orla discovered it through her persistence: Meia prefers women if you please.

We live with responsibilities; countries thrive on chaos. Ruined lives for personal gain.
The Geneva Convention ignored again. The Army's band of brothers; watch your back.
Deployed to join throngs of dysfunctional people, grooming allies; heroes hope to help.
Lads finding joy in diverse ways; losses still cause grief, torture for those who stay.

Hostility skirmishes with truth vying for supremacy; what we are V what we say.

People full of hope, changing how love plagues, plays us; that unavoidable fate,

here to stay. Who can live a better life deprived of love in all its ways? So, Meia's gay.

Individuals now able to select their own ID. Makes for better health to save sanity … REFORM.

Turmoil settles down like the earth that surrounds my friend; whose battle now

is done. We trained, travelled, fought and fretted over everything we did; then some.

If we're ever fortunate enough to have a son we'll call him Raymond, after my chum.

Meia's chasing a degree at university along with her new-found female revelries.

*

MEIA

As Daddy's little darling I grow up; when he's around, gifts and fuss abound.

Mum's a rock till something changes; I'm upside down as childhood slides aside.

Through school I'm nobody's fool for sure. I'll never take any challenge lightly.

BUT: when my mum and dad decide to divorce I think my world has ended.

I'm an amenable child with a bright future I hear, but l grew up with lonely fear.

I'm not alien to love; it once was there. An observation: humans thrive on despair.

There are plenty of friends to meet my ends through life's little ups and downs.

From a haven where I'm spoilt rotten to insecurity and despair, life's a bitch.

My studies were sincere, my grades secure, the world's my oyster so there.

The gifts bestowed on me merited a place in university. I have no plans as yet.

There's change afoot at home; something's gone wrong, nobody said a thing.

A secret service you would think. I don't count as a confidant. *Well*? Is it Dad then?

'I'll miss you my little darling till I come back.' Not to Mum did he say that.

Mum seems to be miles away; overlooking both of us, always deep in thought.

It never crossed my mind to ask there and then: Mum, Dad, what's going on?

I'm in my teens, things are happening. I need guidance but there is none.

I'm not responsible for what I don't understand; I ask my mates, get a hand.

We have a ball playing blind man's buff; when you're caught you get them off.

So it goes on, this curiosity grows strong, I caught a girl, oh fuck, what's wrong?

Finding I'm in the grip of exposure, she shuns my disclosure. How do I carry on?

Taking my temper out on Mum; she's the one to consider, sort things out.

She is no help; needs it herself. Well the hell, eff 'em all. I can't cope at all.

The weed was good as we hit the street, the shops easy targets for a thief.

Kerb crawl, clubbing into the wee small hours, sleepovers; escape routes.

Our time out was spent playing devil's advocate with and for all our friends.

But when my dad was close to death I lost the incentive to lead the squad.

His mate Raymond was dead. Mum was there to see him, but Orla was the

prime one. I lost position as his little precious; Mum done zip to help this.

As time went on I grew livid. How dare this bloody Orla flack me; with my

dad she ends up living. We are stuck in the back of beyond with my gran …

I don't belong; she gets a quantity of grief, now we get the heave. So long.

Mum is suicidal; who gives a shit? Brings me here against my will; this cesspit.

Mum met this guy, he's going to help her finances as well; not if I can help it!

Make a play for him I do; but he shoots me down and that for me is new.

I can't stand that bitch Orla, she's just a man eater; her claws are in my dad,

she's after him for all I ever had. Love and affection; my security lessened.

Mum is courting that bloody Aiden; well, she's working in his firm, flirting.

She needs money – right, it's tight. Me, Meia; I stole lots from her alright.

I've let my dad know where we stand; that cow Orla stepped in, questioning.

What's going on? Where, who, why; and when are you going to grow up?

My mum and Orla made a pact; I can see my dad on their terms, his blessing.
Every time I step out of line; I've now to visit the psychological witch in my life.
My days of men and mayhem are coming to a close, the evil streak is shrinking;
they explain the way it goes. Uni for a spell, settle down, make life worthwhile.

Visiting Orla in our old home; makes her a right thorn, I lay down the law.
I'm full of contempt, resentment. Then Orla asks me about my choice.
'He's my dad. What do you care?' 'We're here because of love or leave,
Meia.' I know rejection is a fatal feeling. For my dad's attention I'm waiting.

In due course I spill my guts; Orla the Ogre's not such a witch or bitch.
Said she can afford to be choosy and tactless but she chose my dad.
Tells me her parents are in danger should she return home to Belfast.
I reach the right conclusion; with composure comes Orla's confession.

Most men can't think past their dick; women are quick but I'm on their
side for what is right. I had my share and to be fair found my forte in
females, what folly. These values, goals and ethics of life are a high price.
Out of the closet it's set me free, what a great time I'll have being me.

I stole, lied at gran's; lonely old hag had no past, now I know. I'm sorry.
I've discovered a lot about the people that matter, the lives I've shook;
shattered, fixing mine. Aiden – Mum marry; for a bum, I suppose he's OK.
Ace courses I choose at uni, they want me to go. I'm away; I rest my case.

Its computers attracting my intellect; a lot sinking in swiftly, I'm sorted.
We're different from each other after all; some folks may not live on lies
behind closed doors, when one does, ultimately innocents pay the price.
Truth was alien to me, life sucking honesty from the lonely and grieving.

Dad and Orla have come a long way; she has commitment, we're sure.
They got the house to help his condition. He talks now, and I listen.
I'm chief bridesmaid at the wedding, Orla's expecting! They'd love a son.
Imagine me with a baby brother. *'Hi Raymond, it's me, Meia: your sister.'*

*

ORLA

I'm a psychologist by day treating deranged; troubled minds and Ulster rages on.
Evenings I escort elites, emotionless please, info leaks. Cracked clients warn me LEAVE.
Blackmail; a dirty word, my parents held hostage. Trusting a traitor; my covert life, it's over.
Crossing the Irish Sea with a new ID. I meet Melvin; the pain of love grows, Meia's a problem.

Great with minds I'm gentle; kind, allowing phantoms of fear to unwind, takes time.
In contrast charged rich fat cats by the hour for services rendered; no rush there then.
Not hypnotising but fraternising, hard as nails I was; they were men of course. Paying
hostage fees to powers that be. My parents in captivity. I fucked one client too many.

I'm easy on the eye: got great cleavage and crotch, brains, a rewarding career.
Reconstructing remnants of disturbed minds; clients, the victims of the times
grew to trust me, warn me I'm being tailed by traitors. Consequently I'm off.
Closing the door to my past; I'm in a class of my own, worth a second chance.

With audacity, wherewithal, a new ID. I'm out on an Irish ferry, won't look back,
not me. My parents know my personal forte lay with married men, no obligation.
They think I'm with my aficionado, his wife will be pleased finding I'm history.
He'll find another lover, it's his forte. I've had several myself, excessive pressure.

So! I'm a spoilt brat in the grip of all that can be bought; except freedom to return.
Impulsive pillow talk with psychology as my profession, a regrettable decision.
Taking all for granted; great clientele, but for what I found out they should dwell in hell.
No regrets; money protects from the troubles. Tormented families driven demented.

Nursing wounded soldiers is now my new career through empathy with my past.
Tasks shock; maimed, mangled remains of human beings mend, or deploy to a military
mortuary. Melvin's a patient I tend in the UK. Intuitively he's alluring to my intellect.
His silence I treasure. Another blathered under no illusion: cost of betrayals, mayhem.

There's post-traumatic stress, forgetfulness. A one to one for this soldier is best.
Wounds may take years to mend, memories constant torment; when will it end?
Melvin's in a place of descent, no sign of family concern. Let healing commence.
Discretion is the greater part of valour; I'll win him over or my names not Orla.

Infrequent visits from Kizzy; she's not trying to reach her man, his daughter rants.
I'm fathoming all aspects of this family's physical and psychological damage.
Meia she came out of the blue with language to match the scenario, what bravado.
Knowing Melvin can't handle this, I chase away the little miss; come again if you're civil.

Melvin's aware of the incident; no reproach, he knows I'm protecting my interest.
Not distressed; he holds my hand close to his chest. Melvin speaks my name, 'Orla.'
We need to resolve this family rejection; I'm egotistic here, my affair. Kizzy, Meia;
what a pair, for Melvin they don't seem to care. I'll be his voice, life, love; his wife.

Falling in love makes a mockery of the way I'm living. Tell him all from the beginning.
I'll fight to be by his side through thin, thick. I'll have to get past his wife and his kid.
How presumptuous: impulsive daydreaming about a future with Melvin. Can it exist?
Shrapnel from land mines killed his friend, shredded him. When will all this evil end?

It can start with an offer of help; building bridges of support for the man I adore.
Meia's dad and I, we're an item, a fact I'll instil in his daughter as I bring her into line.
Melvin can talk, make contributions. We devise a plan. No one will come to harm.
We need Kizzy to comply, her permission we accepted, received with thanks.

Again I revert to psychology; Meia and me alone. I'll open avenues of use.
Kizzy becomes a comrade, relieved her wanton child may find a way to uni.
Released from cords of guilt and rejection, Aiden finds Kizzy employment.
Patience V patient – militant Meia's smarmy vowels; foul manners unveil.

Meia still shuns the frame, we all feel the same: tame, before Aiden and Kizzy wed.
All parents' discord leads to retaliation; the same psychology for every generation.
Where harmony's restored by two or more, I'm on the level but Meia's sceptical.
Skilfully refined is her deception. I won't go away, I'm here to stay; Meia wants to play.

Meia's derogatory values diminish as I integrate my life in the land of troubled souls.
Weeks later relieved participants see improvement; Meia's fraying round the edges.
The vacated home, healing in familiar settings; Melvin's cared for more than I knew.
It's said true love makes the fool of everyone; come join in, it's all fun.

Time, patience, tons of pluck. Meia really sucked, a lesbian afraid to leave the closet.
Did anyone clock it? Secrets cost years of heartache; sorrow detrimental to sanity.
Revealing the truth cleans slates; planning ahead, she gets to visit, talk to her dad.
Winning a place in uni, Meia takes to technology; true friends. Kizzy and Aiden marry.

I'll propose to Melvin; tell him I'm pregnant. Confess to a past; hope for a new start.
Delighted with my request, YES! We'll have a son called Raymond. Discard the rest.
But … before? My ID, lifestyle. My soldier said, 'Before? It's over.' Can't say more.
My parents meet Melvin. Kizzy, Aiden accept an invitation. Meia's chief bridesmaid.

My true ID is sorted out. It put paid to the informer, he won't get another £ from me.
Behind closed doors my tortured speechless treasure, together we made things better.
Melvin and I created this legacy of love; Raymond, he'll arrive when he's ready. OK,
he may become a soldier, psychologist; or follow Meia into technology. Some day!

Lady with Edelweiss

By Steph Newham

'I'm a painter. Unless I've sold a canvas, then I call myself an artist; questionable I know, but it gives me pleasure to say it. Artist. I've not sold much lately, so just now I'm a painter.' I stopped, waiting for her to comment but she didn't. 'You comfortable?' I asked. I watched her shift on the couch. 'We don't own our bodies.' I heard my voice, insistent, patiently repeating the words. 'We don't own our bodies.' I knew if I raised my eyes, I'd meet her stare, see her refusal to let her mind follow the idea I was suggesting. Was it too painful to imagine? Did she think I'd bought her body, not just the right to paint her? 'Here, catch.'

It was so bloody cold, that first day. Winds gale force. A big fucking draughty window. Put the robe on. So soft, it had to be real silk. Who else had worn it?

Sometimes I still catch a flash of speculation in her eyes. Seven months she's been sitting and still doesn't trust me. Wonders why I want to paint her. Wonders just what am I paying for. Wonders why the tattooed edelweiss attracted me. If I gave it a bit of thought I'd be able to answer her, but why waste time thinking about gut feelings when I need to paint.

No matter. I feel a twitch in both palms as I study her. Mounds of flesh; armpit flesh merging with boob flesh always stirs me. It takes a lot of calming breath to get into the work; long moments of empty staring before I add new splurges onto the gessoed surface. I work on, contemplate the curves and angles as she grows on the canvas. I'm tempted to say, 'Chill, I don't go for women with kids and history.' But I don't; I hand over £20 and call it a day.

So now you come each morning, 11 till I'm done. You bathe in the light flooding through the studio skylights. It makes you pallid – pallid but not ugly. Each layer of paint I apply, strips you bare to the bone; creates tension, like the tension that grows the longer one delays making love. I get spiteful. If I feel grumpy, I tell her the crusty mole on her pubes has no business there, it's some sort of strange sign that only a lover should see. Mostly I work in silence.

She thinks I'm ignoring her. Fuck, I'm working. Working on finding out what she's made of. She's more than that indigo tattoo. Edelweiss. Why edelweiss? She's faux leather and eyeliner, smells of incense, sandalwood and jasmine … she's pale, indoors too much. Grey shadows under her eyes; dehydrated? Drinks?

Concentrate, fathead … flesh tones, mmm, cadmium yellow, ultramarine, crimson lake. I wonder if she knows I mix her skin tone; no squeezing a tube to exude a shitty pink. Skin's hard, difficult to get it right. I build it up, layer by layer, each layer a sliver of mind. My mind, her mind, our minds. A tattoo of minds. Interleaved. Nowhere to hide. God she's good, I knew she would be. What if I can do this? Expose her to the world. And herself; does she know why she wanted an edelweiss? It's not really the tattoo; it's her, a jewel under all that flesh.

I love this feeling of insinuating myself under her skin; my mind sinking into her, through the epidermis, down a follicle. Every day's a fresh exploration. New tubes of paint strangulated to flesh out her flesh. Build the bulk of her until she's yielding into the canvas. Scan her soul. Rape her with paint, find out why: why that indigo edelweiss?

'Enough, sun's too low. You're turning gold. Tomorrow? Elevenish?'

He's crazy but I like coming now. I like the inner peace that I get from modelling for him. I empty my mind of all thoughts. Ha! Inner peace – Christ, I'm even beginning to sound like him. Trouble is, it's boring, especially when I'm gagging for a fag. I want to say, 'You're fucking crazy!' You lay me down, then stand back and stare. What kind of man does that? I'd feel OK if you looked like you wanted to screw my brains out. Christ, you make me nervy.

One day he left me, went to answer the door; I looked at his work, canvases stacked against the walls. He's seen it all: wrinkles, mastectomy scars, grey pubic hair, lactating breasts, soggy bottoms, shaved muffs. And tattoos. He's got a thing about them. It pays more 'n a quick shag up an alley wall, but it's more fucking scary.

I can strip off now, lay back, let him move me how he wants. He's not a creep – he's decent. Fussy git. Doesn't like a full bush; sent me to a salon to get waxed.

'A landing strip or shaved off,' he said. 'You'll develop confidence. Own your sexuality and grow in stature.'

'Fuck me, like leeks on a bed of manure,' I said. He didn't laugh. He's kind. If it's going well, he gives me extra. A tenner for the kids, sometimes 20.

'Treat yourself,' he said. *Once the rent's paid and there's food in the cupboard, I get something – a new lippy, lacy knicks – he never notices.*

He moves on bare feet, pushes back my hair with cool hands. Everything is cool here. He says it's the north light falling from high windows. My skin shivers where he's traced a finger over my tattoo.

I didn't answer when he said, 'You like doing this now?'

I nearly said, I've got my benefits sorted, stuff you. But he was grumpier than usual, so I kept it zipped. But I'd be lying. I like it here. I like him looking at me. His eyebrows meet on the bridge of his nose when it's going wrong; it's wrong now. Christ, I hope it's better than the last two. I hold my breath, raise and lower my diaphragm like he's shown me. Relaxxxx. Blood stabs in my bloody forehead, I need to close my eyes; can't he hear my muscles screaming for him to finish for the day? He's unbearable, a bastard. I'm getting my benefits so why do I put up with it?

She's got an arse like the Venus of Willendorf, barely a fold at her waist. She's a satyr raised on its hind legs, mocking me. Taunting me to look into her. Invade.

If I ask her to close her eyes, she takes a deep breath, fights to relax. After all this time, five paintings; doesn't she know I don't even see her nakedness? What I see is the indigo depth of that flower. Wherever my eyes settle on her body, its indigo depths hover just out of reach.

The transparency and opacity of it splurge on my palette. I'm lost in colour saturation; the drip-drip of oil, the slice of a knife through impasto. She still fascinates me, holds a pose indefinitely; not easy. This one's crap – it's too minimal, not really her. It's empty. Destructive deconstruction.

Silence makes people want to talk; she wants to talk. I make no sense to her; she's twitchy, wonders why no sex. I'm her messenger of death – no sex, no food, no life – she's said enough for me to see that. How many words must I spit out before she understands this is work. She works for me. I pay. She splays her thighs and keeps fucking still. Not much to ask, even when my silence presses hard on her.

Most sessions, especially in winter, I earn my cash. Shivering miserably for an hour while I hold a pose.

'Lie on your back – legs up the wall,' he says.

My muscles are on fire. His gaze is intimate, as he scratches yet another me onto yet another canvas in silence. There are no eyes but his and those canvases facing the wall; like he's put us in the naughty corner. He's breathing me in, sucking my soul, swallowing it in saliva behind thin lips. I wish he'd talk more. I like his voice, it's like, low; no, mumbling, like a tube train on the Bakerloo.

I try 'robe drop' moments, a slow reveal; totally wasted on the prat. Not surprising; I had nasty skin infections as a kid. Left me a scarred body. I don't hate it – it's paid the bills. But I don't like it. He's seen more of it than most. More than my last partner. It's not a real relationship, this painting lark, but more than I got with the quick shaggers. He says canvas is the interpreter – 'a silent communicator of oil slick communion' – with what? Not with me, mate. He's on his own trip; oils, pastels, dusty pigments.

'My history written in indigo on your arm,' he says. He talks bloody crap sometimes. He also said I, 'looked like a mobster's moll.'

I said, 'You've got a missing tooth but who's caring.' Not me.

He says, 'You're meant to be available, yet not available.' No idea what he means, but my guts churn. He shouts, 'Give your fucking self.' No – more distant. He's too close, he's electric; making me twitch. 'No, no, no, no, no!' he screams, 'relax, breathe.' His voice deepens, 'Calm, calm, be calm Lady with Edelweiss.' My pulse slows.

We're getting nowhere. He's getting nowhere. I say he, 'should start something else – or get another model.'

He shouts, 'What do you know – this is the one I'm submitting!'

Aw hell, I'm stiff! Three hours; he'd better pay extra if he wants to finish it. Fat lady with tattoo, that's what he's painting. No, he won't call it that. It's bleeding freezing in here and it stinks; must remember to ask if I can bring some incense sticks. I still wonder, why me?

When he prodded my tattoo he said, 'Can I paint you?' Just like that. Half way up that dead escalator we were, I'd stubbed my toes on the sharks' teeth treads. Fucking dangerous. Catching my breath I was, when he touched me. Bloody touched me. Put a finger on my tattoo, pushed in deep. Lucky I didn't nut him. Bit impossible, climbing like that.

I yelled, 'Press a bit harder why don't you mate? Feel some real fucking flesh.'
We were clear of the escalator by then. I stood there, his lemony smell right in my face
and an endless slug of commuters trailing past us. And him with his bloody finger still
attached to my tattoo. Five O'clock, Waterloo station, right at the top of a dead
escalator.

That's when he asked me, 'Is that an edelweiss? Lady with Edelweiss, can I paint
you?'

I remember thinking, why not mate, call it what you like, but a shag's a shag and
I've got two kids to feed. It was a shock getting paid for nothing.

It's finished. He's already started another. Full bush for this one. I didn't notice
for a long time, but he's stopped asking, 'Why an edelweiss?' When I asked why, he said,
'Because I believe in the power of mystery.'

Ha! That made me laugh. Mystery, me? I'm no fucking mystery. No money, well a
bit more nowadays and a bonus if he sells me. Still only two kids. No longer shagged out
– still hoping one day the slow robe drop will work for him; and me.

This one isn't going well. I'm not concentrating. But it'll sell – she sells. Bloody
RA. It's been weeks; not cheap to apply. They don't make it easy. Maybe I should have
focused more on background, been a bit edgier. And how the hell are you meant to decide
on a sale price; how do I price our time, the cost of framing and the RA's 30%
commission? Fuck it; would £80,000 be too unreasonable, Sir?

'Welcome Madam …'

What the fuck's got into him? He's popping a cork and shoving a glass at me.

'We've done it!' He's dancing with himself like a prick on skunk. Then he pulls a
letter out of his sleeve, waves it under my nose, yells, 'I am pleased to inform you that
your work has been selected,' and grabs my glass of plonk which I've hardly had time to
taste and twirls me into the chair. 'Head back, look at the ceiling – one leg over the arm.
OK, that's it … so, Lady with Edelweiss,' he says from behind his easel, 'we have a date:
Burlington House, Piccadilly in June.'

*

'Lady with Edelweiss – stupid bastards, they've hung you too high. Or perhaps not. Who
knows what wisdom there is in a crowd. Do you remember the crush that gave you to
me? A collective offering from the bowels of the earth with its stale breath. Now, I offer

you to … Christ knows … but someone will buy you. A rich Swiss wanker, a collector of edelweiss or nudes.'

The impulse to kiss her came suddenly. I resisted, didn't relish being slapped at the opening night of the Royal Academy's Summer Exhibition. Instead, I took her arm, steered her through the throng of penguined stiffs and birds of paradise flaunting their Stella McCartney and Karl Lagerfeld frocks. Oohing and aahing in unison, all nodding sagely as if they knew each painting's soul intimately.

'You're trembling, more champagne? A canapé? Come away. View yourself from a distance,' I say. I traced my finger over her tattoo, hoped it felt like a caress. 'You and me here, we're just a point in time. An indigo blot.' I pressed my finger into her arm. 'I'll bleed into the past – but you, Lady with Edelweiss, you will endure; hung on a wall, unchanging. Let's go.'

I took a last look over my shoulder, saw myself staring down at the twats. I felt a moment's sadness that I'd scarred my beautiful body with a tattoo, but if I hadn't, I wouldn't be twining fingers with a painter; a gap-toothed painter who was going to shag me … very soon.

Against All Odds

By Kath J. Rennie

Family and friends applaud as Mike and I enter the hotel's grand hall. I'm lost for words. Banners decorate the walls. Red heart-shaped balloons float above the tables. The room feels oppressive to me; I really don't want to be celebrating my 40th wedding anniversary here.

'Who the hell's done all this, Mike? Because, believe you me, I'll be having words with the family if it's them and not the staff. It's over the top! And tacky!'

'I can't believe what you just said, Mary. What on earth's wrong with you, woman? Granted you're on edge, but bloody hell. You need to calm yourself down, or you and I will fall out.' He takes my arm firmly and leads me through the guests to the same table we shared on our honeymoon all those years ago.

I can't do this Mike! Don't make me! Don't you remember why we spent our honeymoon here after the death of the babies?'

'Of course I remember, you daft cow! I'm feeling it as well, you know. For God's sake, get a grip. Give me that gorgeous smile of yours, and act surprised! You aren't supposed to know about this party. Or about the kids inviting those so-called parents of yours.'

I give a wry smile. 'Why the hell would they come, anyway? We've not spoken for years!'

'Probably heard that you're in the money,' he jokes. 'Winning that dress design contract made you headline news.'

'Well … they're in for a shock; they are! They'll not get one penny!'

'Fucking right they won't!'

I fondle the locket Mum gave me the day she walked out of my life. I sometimes think we could make things better between us. *Ha! That will be the day. She's never shown any remorse. Does she feel any? And Dad – will he have the brass neck to show his face?*

I choke back tears. If I cry I'll not be able to stop; my mascara's not waterproof. *Don't cry Mary ... Don't, you, dare, cry!* I repeat the silent mantra as Mike clasps my hand firmly.

'Whatever the night brings, sweetheart,' he assures, 'I'm by your side. Always have been, always will be.'

'I know you will.' I'm finding it hard to breathe.

'You alright? You've gone whiter than white!'

'I'm okay,' I lie.

The guests encourage us to make our way to the centre of the dance floor. Mike more or less pulls me along. My high heels clickety-click on the oak flooring. Everyone's watching – I wish I hadn't worn my four-inch Prada shoes. Or this dress. A heel catches in the hem; I swish the black silk free, scared to death I'll trip.

'I wish I was in jeans and a top.'

'You look a million dollars! It's great to see you looking all glam. Now come on, give everyone that smile of yours.' He twirls me away and pulls me back in time with the music.

And I smile. It's bravado. I hate being the centre of attention and I can't stop glancing at the hall door. *Pull yourself together woman! Try and enjoy yourself. But what if they don't come? Last thing we heard, Mum's been poorly. How will you feel then?*

I remember the pain I felt all those years ago when Mum left Dad and me: her at the front door, one of Dad's friends putting her suitcase in his car. I remember screaming, 'Where are you going? You can't leave us.' Dad was calling his mate a traitorous bastard and he hoped he'd burn in hell.

Mum certainly burnt with him – on Jamaican beaches. For a while she sent me letters and photographs. I wrote back, but stopped when I got a letter telling me she was pregnant.

I hope she doesn't turn up. I don't want them here tonight.

I feel my stomach churn. Mike takes me into his arms.

'Come on, darling, relax.'

'That's easier said than done,' I reply.

'How will the girls feel,' he says, 'seeing you so worked up? And okay, they've made a mistake inviting that lot! But look what they've done for us.'

'It's thoughtful of them. But what are they expecting to happen tonight? A miracle of some sort?'

He slides a finger down the side of my face, lifts my chin to meet his eyes. Brushing my fringe aside, he says, 'I do understand how you feel, Mary. I know being back at this hotel is getting to you, but love, we're here now. Let's try and enjoy ourselves.'

He cups my face in his calloused hands, hands which have worked tirelessly to provide a comfortable home for our sons. Then he places his lips on mine. Lightly at first, but they remain for longer than my embarrassment can cope with. His friends shout out, 'Get a room!' Mike, never a shy man, smiles his cocky smile.

How I wish we could be alone together and shut the rest of the world out.

We're interrupted by our granddaughter who pulls at my gown. I lift her up, smother her with kisses. It calms me. I cuddle her until her mother takes her away. Mike takes the opportunity to give the disc-jockey the thumbs up to begin his set.

The disc-jockey's an old friend of Mike's; he congratulates us and dedicates the first song, 'Only You' by The Drifters, to 'the best couple in the room, Mary and Mike'. Everyone applauds us, then the music starts. Mike cosies up, whispers in my ear, 'Our sons know us so well. Our favourite song. Do you remember when the band played it for us on the first night of our honeymoon here?'

'Yes I do,' I whisper back. Tears well up as Mike sings the opening lines of the song, serenading me. The words transport me back in time, to our first encounter.

*

Mrs Hilda Alshaw's haberdashery shop was tucked away in a Manchester back street. Mum was a frequent visitor: 'to buy some wool,' she would tell Dad. But he said, 'it's to bloody gossip. I expect you'll be talking about me behind my back, saying I'm no use to you! You think it's easy for me, stuck most of my time in this chair.'

Dad went on to accuse her of neglecting him and having a fella on the side. *But who would blame her if she did?* Most of the time he ignored her, hiding behind his newspaper or escaping down the yard to his pigeon loft. Things changed for me that

Saturday when Mum came home and told Dad that she'd found me a job at Mrs Alshaw's.

'Our Mary's too delicate to work in the cotton mill, like you wanted her to, or at that bleeding biscuit factory. And don't give me that look! You'd still have a job if you'd not gone into work hung-over.'

'Good for her! About time the lazy cow got off her arse and found out what it's like to do proper work, day in and day out. Not like you, sitting at that sewing machine for hours on end. The bloody noise drives me mad.'

'You selfish, rude bastard! Me sitting at that machine puts food in your belly.'

And beer, I wanted to add, but didn't dare.

Dad ignored her remark. 'She wears me down with her fanciful dreams … "I'm going to be a designer! I'll have my own business one day." She's got ideas above her station, that one, just like you!'

The argument continued. I fled to my bedroom and smothered my ears with my pillow.

The next day they were back to ignoring each other, but Mum carried on telling me about the job; she said that I was replacing someone who'd been sacked for taking days off. They had been caught after phoning in sick then being spotted walking in Piccadilly Gardens. It was funny hearing Mum mimic her friend.

'The girl got me good and proper. She must have held her nose when telling me over the phone she had flu. I believed her!'

Mum said Mrs Alshaw had gone on and on. Said she couldn't keep the window display nice. Customers would pass by. Said she'd hang up her apron if she couldn't find another girl.

'She thinks her shop's too small, says they all want to work in the big ones, the better-paying places! I said to her, "Could my Mary work for you? She's good with the sewing machine. She makes her own clothes. She's a good girl; I'll see she's on time."'

And that was it. I had a job and would start the following week.

*

The shop looked old fashioned and run down. It smelt musty. So did my boss. I felt like a soldier on parade as she inspected me from top to toe.

'Mary, did you … tut! Did you make that outfit? Tut!'

'Yes! Don't you like it? It's trendy.'

'The skirt's very … umm … short!'

'It's supposed to be. It's a mini-skirt. Everyone's wearing them.'

'Well, my girl, I'm surprised at your mum letting you wear something so revealing. But then I've noticed she's showing all she's got these days.' Mrs Alshaw handed me a khaki overall. 'You'll be dressing that window. We can't have everybody stopping and staring at you.' She pointed towards the threadbare mannequin in the shop window.

'Now, dearie. I want you to make a dress and put it on her. Not a short one like yours. Out back you'll find rolls of materials; choose a nice one. I want her elegant, mind. Her wooden pole's a bit wobbly and wood-wormed, but don't worry, they don't bite! You'll find hats in boxes in the back.' She pulled out a drawer underneath the counter. 'In here are all the bits and bobs you'll need.'

'I've never window-dressed before! I can't do that,' I stammered.

'Don't underestimate yourself, girl. We never know what we can do until we try.'

'Please let me stay behind the counter. I only make clothes for myself and Mum, and I've never used a dummy.'

'Don't you dare call her a dummy, Mary. I'll have you know many a fine outfit has been made on her. She's been with me since I opened this shop. She's a part of it. I know she's a bit worn. I would have taken a needle and thread to her myself, but for my damned arthritis. It grieves me, her getting *sooo* cold. If you want to work here, dearie, I suggest you get started.'

I made my way into the storeroom. I had to clear the cobwebs and dust off the materials. They were beautiful, bright silks, wool tartans, and pretty cottons. I was amazed, given Mrs Alshaw's drab appearance, always dressed from head to toe in black.

Remembering Mrs A's comment about my mini-skirt, I drew a sketch of a trendy maxi-dress. Hippie-style, a longer length; I was sure this would also hide the wooden pole, which I'd scrutinised for anything wriggling about.

I measured the mannequin's bust, waist and hips. It annoyed me that it had no arms or head. No head? How was I supposed to give it a hat to wear?

When I mentioned this problem, Mrs A said, 'Use your head, girl!'

I hated working in the window, hated people watching me, but I tried to ignore them. I was determined to make a good job of the mannequin and the window display. Hopefully Mrs A would let me serve behind the counter once it was done. The head was a problem, but I asked Mrs A's permission to use skeins of white wool; I shaped them until they resembled a head, which I taped onto the mannequin's neck. Finally, I covered the head in white chiffon.

'Look Mrs A!' I said proudly. 'Look, she's got a head.'

I expected praise. All I got was, 'Stop bragging, girl and get on with the job. You haven't got all day.'

Grinding my teeth, I attached a floppy straw hat, wound a wide yellow ribbon round the brim and tilted it sideways to give it a chic look. *You poor moth-eaten thing! I wonder, could I give you button eyes? Nah! I'm not doing any more. It's too hot – and I've had enough of being stared at like I'm under a microscope. Nosey gits!*

Spurred on, I wound the cornflower silk I'd chosen round the top half of the dummy; then I pinned yellow ribbons, the same colour as the hat, to the bottom half of a silky dress Mrs A said I could use. It fell in folds covering the pole.

'You're doing well there Mary!' Mrs A said, coming from behind the counter to see how I was doing. 'I made that old dress for a customer but I botched the top half. About time it was put to good use.'

I was proud of what I'd achieved, and I'd been oblivious to the knocking on the window-pane. Now I turned to see a crowd of young men peering up at me.

'Hey darling,' one of them shouted, 'your legs are better than the dummy's.'

Of course they are, I wanted to reply. *Mine aren't made of wood!* I felt my face burn. I wanted to escape.

'Ignore them!' Mrs A said. 'Take no notice. They'll soon lose interest and go and bother somebody else.'

She was right. They all walked away – except one. I took a few glances at him. He was at least six-foot tall, dressed in dirty, torn-at-the-knees jeans and a black leather jacket with a sleeveless denim jacket over it. He grinned and turned his back to me, showing off an emblem sewn onto it. My breath caught in my throat as I realised he was part of a gang I'd heard so much about … Hells Angels.

When he turned back, our eyes met. He flicked his long fringe out of his blue eyes. I felt like a fly caught in a spider's web – I couldn't move! I looked down to his knee-length biker boots; to his hands and the helmet he carried. He placed his puckered lips on the window-pane. I wanted to kiss them, but Mrs A shouted at me.

'Mary, get out of that window and back to the counter.'

I made to escape, but tripped, knocking the mannequin over. I caught it in time, but the head fell off. *Fuck!*

Out on the street the Angel howled with laughter. I scowled and gave him the V sign. He winked at me.

'Bugger off!' I bellowed.

'Don't lose your head,' he yelled back.

Giggling, I picked up the head and fastened it back on the mannequin. I turned to give him a smug smile, but he'd gone. The street was empty.

I felt miserable as I joined Mrs Alshaw behind the counter.

'That's not a bad job you've done, Mary. It's taken you longer than it should have, mind you. That boy, Michael Hunt, took your attention. He's a bad one! He's got a terrible reputation.'

Who cares! I like him! I thought as I watched Mrs A winding a roll of ribbon and sliding it on a pole with lots of others on a shelf at the back of the counter.

'I'm not one to gossip, dearie, but apparently he's had as many girlfriends as I've had hot dinners.' She picked up another length of ribbon. 'Here, roll this one. He's not the settling-down type. He's been out of control, that one, ever since his poor mother went to join my Albert. Up there.' She pointed to the ceiling. 'And his father chucked him out. Don't know what for.' Her tone changed. 'Now, don't you be fooled by him, because he's just walked through the door. I'll serve him, dearie. You get on with these ribbons.'

My knees were trembling. What's he up to, I thought as I dropped the ribbon onto the counter, bobbed down quickly and pretended to tidy a drawer.

'Can I help you, laddie?' I heard Mrs A say. 'I hope you've not come in just to bother my assistant.'

Ignoring Mrs A, my Mr Right heaved himself up and leant over the counter. 'Hi there gorgeous; are you snubbing me?'

I stammered, 'I was just … putting a box of buttons … away in the bottom drawer.'

'Are you sure about that now? It looked as though you were snubbing me.'

'Now why would I do that, Sir?' I blushed as I stood up. I'd been told to address everyone as sir or madam.

'Sir, is it? Aren't you the polite one! Call me Michael. Mike for short.'

'What can I help you with? Mike.'

Mrs A poked me in the ribs, but I stood my ground.

'Have you got any more of that blue ribbon that you put on the dummy?'

'We have,' I said, 'it's the same colour as your eyes.' *Oops! Did I say that? Shit! Did I really say that?* But I must have done, because Mrs A pushed me out of the way, much to my Angel's amusement.

'Do you want a length of ribbon? Or not?' she demanded. But Mike ignored her.

'I'll have bright red,' he said, smiling at me. 'Same colour as your beautiful cheeks. I bet there's been a few fellas kissed them peaches.'

Mrs A marched across the shop and opened the door wide. *Spoilsport! I'm having fun. What would she know of love at first sight?*

'I don't let any fella kiss me!' I said. 'Not until I get to know them better.' *Oh hell! What am I doing? He'll think I'm easy.*

'Oh, is that right?' he said, a sparkle in his eyes. 'Well then, how do you fancy meeting me at the Odeon at seven this Friday night? Don't be late!'

He sauntered out of the shop and Mrs A slammed the door after him.

Will I meet him? I'm not sure. Of course I will. But I say nothing.

*

That Friday we kissed and cuddled in the back row of the cinema. Every time he took his mouth from mine I was left wanting more, and I knew he wanted more than that. I said no. I wasn't ready. I wasn't going to end up with a shotgun wedding and a baby. We walked home slowly, telling each other all the things we couldn't admit to the world.

That was the turning point in my life. Mike waited outside the shop every evening for me to finish work. Mrs A wouldn't let him inside. We would go to a café: play the juke box and pin-ball machine. Then he'd whisk me off on his bike for a spin, before dropping me off near home. I wouldn't let him park his motorbike anywhere near the house; it would only cause more trouble. And I had trouble already. Every weekend I was making excuses to get out of the household chores.

'What do you mean, you're going out? Where? With who? You've got work to do, girl. You'll stay put!' Mum ranted.

All I looked forward to now was pillioning on Mike's 650 Triumph. Speeding on motorways; enjoying the wind in my hair; not bothering to wear a crash helmet. Being one of the Angels, I loved the sense of danger and freedom. I loved being me. A fiercer, independent woman. I no longer felt like a kid. But sometimes I wished we were free of Mike's friends. His comrades, as he called them.

'Why do we always have that lot hanging round with us?' I moaned. 'Why can't we just go off; pitch our own tent? Be on our own?'

'Wherever I go, as President of the chapter, they have to follow.'

I felt like telling him to get lost, piss off. But I didn't.

I couldn't stay angry with him for long. I enjoyed our time together too much, particularly those times in the sand dunes. We made camp fires and danced around them, and talked into the small hours, before creeping away to our own tent where Mike made passionate love to me, and we fell asleep in each other's arms. My weekends with Mike were magical.

But back at work, I got it in the neck.

'No good will come of it, Mary,' Mrs Alshaw parroted.

I told her, 'He's not what you think he is, Mrs A. He's kind and gentle and he loves me.'

But Mrs A kept on. 'If your mum and dad find out you've been seeing that tearaway, there'll be hell to pay, girl! I don't know how they believe your tales of staying over at a girlfriend's house.'

But I didn't give a shit! Mike talked of me moving into his bedsit. I dreamed I'd become a good seamstress, create outfits for younger customers with money to burn. I was already making changes, boosting Mrs A's sales. Slowly but surely her attitude changed. I came to admire her. I made outfits for her – outfits which made her look more professional and younger. She was grateful, and told me on numerous occasions: 'I look like I did before losing my Albert.' Mrs A and I were becoming real friends.

*

Those days now feel so long ago. I allow myself to be pulled close as our song ends. Then I try to slip from his arms, but Mike's reluctant to let me go.

'Just another dance?' he whispers. I think he still senses my panic, so I nestle my head under his chin and let him hold me tight again. 'We've been very lucky, haven't we, Mary? We've come through thick and thin together – and what a good job we've done with our sons. Who could ask for better boys? Aren't you proud of them?'

'Yes I am,' I say as I look with pride at our sons. 'They're the best. I just wish their wives hadn't interfered; they had no right sticking their noses in by inviting my parents. I don't want to see my mum and dad again.'

'They thought they were doing the right thing, Mary, and you know what? I don't think they'll turn up. It's their loss. Don't fret. And if truth be known, I don't want them here. I'll never forgive them for the way they treated you.'

'You forgave your father,' I say as we make our way back to our table.

'That was different. He asked me to when he was dying. But it's a difficult one with your parents; especially your old man. I can't forget that night I went to ask his permission to marry you.'

'I don't want to think about that night, Mike. Please go and get a round in. I need a brandy. Get me a double. I need it!'

I watch Mike stride across the dance floor; my rock – he's easy with everyone, a smile, and bit of banter. I feel tears welling up again. I'm so damned angry, even though it's been thirty years since Dad threw me out … since I'd lost the babies. I remember Dad screaming at us; me screaming back and Mike trying to do the right thing, telling Dad he loved me, and that selfish bastard just wanting me as a servant. I drain my glass, shudder. I try not to think anymore, but the memory forces itself through: my waters breaking, and Mike leaning me against the gate while he ran and phoned for an ambulance. Then he came back to support me, all the while keeping Dad at arm's length. God, I really thought Dad was going to kill him.

*

Family and friends smooch to the last slow dance of the night. Mike's eager for us to join with them; I try to smile, brush away the tears rolling down my cheeks.

'I'd rather we didn't, Mike. Let's just sit and finish our drinks then say goodbye.' I lift my glass. 'But let's toast ourselves, darling: a good life, good boys, a real family to be proud of.'

We hardly have time to clink our glasses before the guests fall silent and part to allow my darling Mrs A to pass through. She's done up like a dog's dinner and being pushed in a wheelchair by a tall bloke.

'Oh my God!' I gasp. Mike and I jump up; I fling my arms round her neck. 'Mike, did you arrange this?'

Mike laughs. 'No, I think this one is down to those interfering daughters-in-law of yours!'

Now I'm sobbing tears of joy.

'Well, girl,' Mrs A says with pride in her voice, 'you made it to the top. A renowned designer! Sally has already told me that stupid pair of articles that don't deserve to be called parents didn't show up.'

But I don't have time to reply. The guests crowding round part again and there stand my mum and dad. I feel the blood drain from my face.

'You two!' I shriek, as Mike grasps my hand.

'Leave them to me, Mary.'

I'm shaking as he walks over to them.

'So the pair of you think you'll come here tonight and sponge off your famous daughter, do you?'

'Well don't we deserve something?' Dad says smarmily.

He's not changed. I have to tell him so.

'No you fucking don't, Dad,' I howl. I lift my skirt, swagger confidently across to them. 'You deserve nothing. My life is down to Mrs A, and she's my fairy godmother. She gave me what you pair couldn't: love.'

Mum starts crying. 'Mary I'm sorry.' She looks heartbroken. I feel my own heart melt, and pull her into my arms while looking daggers at Dad.

'It's okay, Mum,' I say. 'Yes, you left me, but even when you were on the other side of the world in Jamaica, you only ever wanted the best for me. But you!' I almost spat, turning to Dad. 'Now I finally understand why Mum left all those years ago. She never wanted to leave me. She only wanted to get as far away as possible from you. Get out of here and out of my life!'

The guest's part for the final time and my dad hobbles out of my life.

Mum tries to hug Mrs A, but it isn't over. Mrs A winks at me and Mike, and has a go at Mum. 'Your self-pity doesn't wear with me. I'm still furious with you. Where the hell was you when she miscarried? Eh? I was left to deliver two dead babies and care for her. But,' Mrs A says with a smile, 'you can't keep a good working-class girl down when she's got the knack of using a sewing machine. Probably the best thing you ever did for her was teach her to sew. But that's all you ever did for her. Tomorrow you can make your way back home again, and it'll be up to Mary to decide if she ever wants to see you again.'

I look from Mrs A to Mum and reach out a hand to both of them.

Enough. The past is done with.

'Mum,' I say, 'I hope we can still keep in touch sometimes. Mrs A, I know you'll still always be at the end of the telephone when I need you.'

'Until it's time for me to go up and join Albert.' She points to the ceiling.

I hug her frail body gently, grateful to her for taking us in that night when we turned up at her home, bereft and homeless. Forever grateful for the way she coped with our miscarriage, and for arranging and financing our marriage at Gretna Green.

'Get away to your beds, you soft sods!' she orders. 'Go and make the most of this place's four-poster beds. My treat again. Not that I mind. I just want you both to get my money's worth!'

And after doing as instructed, snuggled in each other's arms, we talk of the expected due date of our twin granddaughters, and a future truly cemented with love.

Number 4 Parliament Street

By Christina Openshaw

In 1880 I was a new house in a new street – Parliament Street, so it said on the wall of the house across – an ordinary two up two down, brick walls, with a flat-fronted sash window amongst a row of others just like me. My front door opened directly onto the pavement that was one step down, but I did have a long backyard with a little brick house at the end, near the gate.

When my family moved in there was Lily, she was only a child then, and her mum and dad. Lily would run up and down my stairs making tip tapping noises with the metal studs on the bottom of her clogs, singing nursery rhymes. Her voice tinkled through my very being; it made me happy. My rooms would be ringing with the sound of laughter, giving me a warm feeling.

Her parents would shout when she did wrong, though she never meant to. Eager to go out to play, she would often leave my front door open. After a telling-off, I felt her heavy footsteps as she ran up to her bedroom, and I would hear her muffled sobs coming from under the pillow. I wished I could wrap my walls around her. Both of us were learning.

Lily started going somewhere called school; she went there a few days every week. I didn't understand why she had to go. With my rooms empty I felt all alone. I missed her not being with me.

Then when she got older, she was still going to school in the morning. In the afternoon she went to work at the mill with her mum. Both coming home tired, they would push my door open slowly, their shoulders stooped. Lily was lacking her usual energy, I felt sorry for them!

Soon, Lily started to go out early with her mum to work, and I wouldn't see her or anyone as often. But I looked forward to the times I did. That's when we were a family again.

Lily was married at 18 to Jim, a miner. I'd watched them since they were small as they played games together in the street. We all lived together happily: Lily, Jim, me and her parents, until they in turn passed away. Each had what they called a funeral, leaving my front room in a box. I watched as it was put on the horse and cart, usually used by the rag and bone man. It went down the street followed by Lily and Jim. She was sobbing so much her whole body shook. Jim put his arm around her to give comfort. I wished I could!

One day I heard Lily making queer grunting sounds in the front bedroom. Jim was pacing back and forth on my flag floors downstairs. His heavy work boots sounded and felt just like the dray horses that went up and down the street, shaking my walls. What's going on, I wondered? Lily shouting – she never did that! Doctor Clark was there and Mrs Smith from next door. Both were dashing about, Mrs Smith running up and down stairs with basins of hot water; what a commotion! Then crying noises I'd never heard before – except when the black and white cat used to sit on the wall outside, calling to another down the street.

It seems we had two babies in the house now: Joe and Sam. This was all new to me. The neighbours dropped in bringing gifts for the boys; twins they called them. Growing up, the lads were both full of mischief with their loud yelling and banging noises echoing through all my rooms, shaking my floors. It was worse when they kicked at my wall with their football or banged my front door playing knock at the door, run! Why do boys have to be so noisy? I prefer the quiet, like it was when Lily was a child.

Even though money was short, all went well as we muddled through life with all its ups and downs. Lily planted a pink rambling rose on the backyard wall; her pride and joy. It was lovely seeing its pretty blooms in the summer. Jim started growing potatoes, carrots and other vegetables in front of the border, enough to feed them all. None of the other houses in the street looked onto such greenery; it made me so proud!

The kitchen would become busy and noisy as I watched the whole family chopping vegetables for soup.

'Mind what you're doing boys,' Lily would say, 'we don't want either of you nicking a finger.'

Then she would push the heavy pan over the fire in the black leaded grate. Delicious cooking smells wafted through all my rooms. I was warm then; it was such a good time!

We all got along merrily with both sons working down the pit with Jim. Each day Lily waved them off – handing them a homemade pasty and a bottle of cold tea for their break. Both of us were so proud! One day the boys, now 17, each got a letter in the post. Lily put them behind the clock on the mantelpiece until they came home from work. She looked unhappy – I think she knew what they were.

They read out their letters – their call up papers – shocked faces from all the family, especially Lily. Call up papers – what are those I wondered?

'You lads won't have to go,' Lily sighed. 'You both work in the pit and are exempt.'

It was not to be. Both wanted to go.

'Do our bit,' they said.

They went to somewhere they called France. I didn't know where that was. It seems there was a war being fought there; they called it the 'Great War'. But something must have happened because the twins never came back.

Feelings here changed then. Lily so distraught, crying all the time, Jim putting his arms around her, holding her close and trying to comfort her. How I would have loved to do that. She and Jim, both heartbroken, drifted along. For them there was no life here, no laughter, no fun, only unhappiness and gloom. I wished they knew I felt their sadness too.

Eventually things here got better. Jim began to grow vegetables once more. Lily started to become more interested in me. She spring cleaned all my rooms, washed my windows and mopped my floors. I was looking better, cleaner and I felt loved again.

But things worsened some years later when Jim, getting older, had a bad accident down the pit. With both legs damaged, he was left bedbound and his bed brought down into the front room. There wasn't much space to move around but Lily would manage; she always did. Spending all her time looking after him, keeping him as comfortable as possible was hard work. Extra washing to do each day, then seeing to his every need took its toll. She was tired; I could tell. I felt for her as she trudged heavily and slowly up and down my stairs. So different from the young Lily I remembered. Even with all her care, Lily and I could see him getting worse. Jim hung on to life a few months before he too died.

'He's with our boys now,' Lily sobbed. I thought this a strange thing to say.

Lily was alone and miserable; this feeling rubbed off on me. Once she had been a house-proud woman, but now my windows were never cleaned so I couldn't see out. My front step never got whitened; we'd both been so pleased with a newly-whitened step. With no rugs beaten on the line and everything dusty, I felt grimy. I saw her turn in on herself, ignoring friends and neighbours, going out to the shops only when necessary. She ate when her stomach rumbled, then just picked at her food. I watched each day as she sat hunched over in her rocking chair, an old shawl around her now skinny shoulders. Looking into the fire, reliving the happy times she and the family shared. I wished I could comfort her.

Eventually she gave up on life, drifted away, alone, unloved; just like me. She left in a box just like her mum, dad and Jim. People came, took everything out of my rooms, leaving me bare. As the years passed, I became more dismal and dilapidated. My woodwork started to peel and my garden was strewn with rubbish. I felt so cold and empty!

One winter night, I became so angry! Children had found a way in – climbing through my small pantry window, bringing with them pieces of wood, even coal to light fires to keep themselves warm. At least this heated me up for a short while. It's a good job my floors were flagged, so not much damage was done. Boys visited nearly every night, banging about noisily – shouting, aggravating the neighbours and me! The police were sent for, cars drew up outside with their flashing lights. The boys tried to get away, but were grabbed by the scruff of their necks; that was funny! They were taken back to their homes to face the wrath of their parents. Next, the police arranged for my doors and windows to be boarded up. I looked even more wretched and I couldn't see out! It was worse than the time Lily didn't clean my windows. I waited, for years I waited …

*

In 1952, John and Ann Bradshaw had the deposit for the empty house they'd seen for sale; that was me. Houses were still in short supply since the Second World War, but the Bradshaws were lucky; no one was ready to take me on in such a poor condition. Would they buy me? Make me look better? I had hope!

Looking around, Ann was thrilled.

'The rooms are bigger than I thought they'd be, don't you think so John? And I'll have the garden I've always wanted. It's even got a Polly Perkins rose growing on the side wall; it's very overgrown, just needs cutting back … I love it!'

I looked forward to them living here, with all their youth and energy, it was just what I needed.

On their next visit, key in hand, John pushed open the door; both were ready to enter. Then, to Ann's surprise, John lifted her up in his arms and carried her over the threshold.

'I never realised you could be so romantic, John,' she whispered. I'd never seen that happen before; how odd these two were!

They walked all around my rooms to decide what jobs needed doing.

John said, 'The floors need replacing first. We'll have to take up these stone flags and lay down concrete before we do anything else.'

I didn't understand – what was wrong with my floors?

'So, it looks like we'll have to wait a while to move in,' Ann sighed. 'It needs a new kitchen and one of those tiled fireplaces to replace the old black leaded range. I wouldn't have liked to use one of those to cook on. There's no bathroom either; can you do that too?'

'Of course, next to the kitchen is a pantry. That's the ideal place to put it,' replied John.

Tiled fireplace, bathroom, what are they? I'll have to wait and see!

Both were so excited to get things started. The following weekend with floor flags taken up, John placed wooden battens in a lattice pattern for the concrete. They laughed as they balanced along these to cross from room to room trying not to lose their footing and fall in. I thought them funny too. Their laughter was rubbing off on me! This was what I'd been waiting for!

John and Ann were out at work throughout the day. All was quiet then, but they worked here every night and weekends – there was lots of banging and crashing in every room. With both friends and family roped in to help, it had never been so busy here since I can't remember when.

It was all worth it in the end! I now had a new tiled fireplace and a bathroom. Even a new window – how much smarter I was! The best thing of all was my brand new shiny blue front door. I'd waited so long for one; and it had a beautiful oval window. Its glass was patterned with funny shaped circles that let a myriad of the sun's rays flood into my front room. They would dance around, lighting up my walls, floors and ceiling. I felt warm again!

John looked pleased at their handiwork.

'Now we need to buy some furniture, maybe a new bed and sofa. We can't afford everything new though.'

Ann nodded. 'We'll have to ask around, see if anyone has anything to spare.'

Within a couple of weeks, they'd collected a dark wood wardrobe with a chest of drawers that didn't match, but that didn't matter. They were given a lighter wooden sideboard, a small kitchen table and four odd chairs; all these from friends and family. They were delighted! I was happy – I was being lived in once more.

'I love our little house now, John.'

'We should hold a party to celebrate, invite all who have helped us. Christmas is coming so we'll have it then.'

'That's a great idea, I'll start to get it organised and make a list.'

A party, fantastic! I hadn't had one here for decades. There were parties along the street when both World Wars ended. But nothing happened here, I'd been so envious.

On party night, the kitchen table groaned under the weight of food, some of it brought along by the revellers. There were sandwiches, sausage rolls, pies and pasties. Homemade cakes and trifles for the sweet toothed. In the centre two cheese-and-pickle hedgehogs; the latest fad at parties, such strange things!

On the side unit stood bottles of sweet sherry and dandelion and burdock; in the corner a barrel of beer for the men. Lots of people filled my front room, some trying to dance to the music playing on the borrowed record player. Sometimes standing on one another's toes as there was hardly any room. My rooms filled with gaiety and laughter. It made me happy to see so many people breathing life into my walls again.

'It's been a great first Christmas, John, with everyone here enjoying themselves. Now we can to get back to normal.'

'Yes, it's been grand,' John said proudly.

Life settled down, both out working, John even doing extra jobs at weekends to build up their bank account. One night, John was fast asleep, dead to the world. Then there was a noise from above. Ann heard it, but it didn't wake John.

'He's had a hard day,' Ann whispered to herself. 'There it goes again!' Ann lay, not moving. Then all went quiet, no noise, just silence. Eventually she drifted off as sleep took hold.

The next morning Ann looked back to the previous night. 'Did I imagine hearing noises? Was I dreaming?' she asked herself, laughing as she put it out of her mind.

I knew; wish I could explain things!

John was working weekends at the home of Mr Davies, owner of the local electrical shop. One Saturday lunchtime, he walked into our house carrying a large box under his arm.

'Oh John, it's a television! Is it for us? I don't know anyone else who has one.'

'Of course it's ours! We'll be able to watch the Queen's coronation in June. That's why I've been working extra hours for Mr Davies.' I wasn't sure what this was all about. Such excitement and so much was happening! It was only a small 10 inch screen television set: His Master's Voice. It was brown with a dog listening to a gramophone pictured on the side. They sat it on the coffee table and John fiddled with the knobs while Ann moved the aerial around as he directed. Then a picture appeared, although not a good one.

'John, it's the Oxford Boat Race! What a shame it's snowing down south right now, even at the end of March.'

'Oh Ann, it's not snowing, the white dots are due to the reception we're getting. You just need to keep the aerial still when I tell you.' They both laughed uncontrollably.

I smiled to myself, but not quite sure if I understood!

On Coronation Day, the front room was bedlam. A bunch of people crowded in; children sat on the floor. Mrs Ball from next door brought chairs and Ann's friend, Sally Harrison, brought some too. Once sat down, no one could move. The curtains were closed as it was better to see the small screen in the dark. There was so much noise at first, then quiet except for the oohs and aahs as they watched open-mouthed at the splendour and pageantry on the screen.

'We could almost be there, it's like seeing it first hand,' said Mrs Ball, so excited she couldn't sit still. All this was new to everyone, making them feeling good. So much fuss, so many people. My walls were bulging.

Weeks later there was a loud knock at the door, Ann answered.

'Hi Sally, come on in.' Ann paused. 'Is something the matter?' she asked and put an arm around her friend.

'It's Dave, Ann. He's seeing someone else.' Sally started to cry.

'Are you quite sure, what makes you say that?'

Between sobs she explained. 'I've thought so for a while, I just had a feeling. He's been going out in the evenings with his workmates, he said. I looked through his clothes in the wardrobe and found a ticket stub for the pictures. We've not been to see a film since I can't remember when.'

'What are you going to do now Sal?'

Sally, a little calmer, answered, 'I've already done it. I've cut up all his clothes. Dave won't be going anywhere soon,' and held up a large pair of scissors. They both started to giggle.

I couldn't understand why. People are such strange things!

Then one night, again noises. Not loud ones, just a quiet scuffling sound, but it didn't last long. I listened to Ann talking to herself.

'Maybe it's next door, either that or it's Lily's ghost?' then she laughed. Ann must have heard the sad story of Lily when she lived here.

I wish I could have eased her mind!

Life drifted along pleasantly. The following year a new baby; a little girl they called Julie. Then everything changed … she seemed to be crying day and night. There was no getting away from it, I wished I could! Hoping it would it all end? It did. Julie ran from room to room and was so full of joy and energy. She took over the whole house – she reminded me of Lily when she was small. Two years later another girl arrived: Beth. She was a much quieter baby and calmer. She didn't keep me awake throughout the night. I liked Beth much better!

Now there were two children in the house growing up together. There was fun, jollity, as well as squabbles. Julie, being the elder was always in charge and more level headed, more grown-up. Beth was always funny and silly, such a turn around since they were babies.

They used my front wall doing handstands, their feet thumping against my bricks and making me shudder. Rubbing along together except for the rows they had, as sisters seem to do. The regular pillow fights over nothing much. Their beds bounced; we could all hear the sound of the bedsprings twanging through the house.

Ann would shout up, 'Be quiet and go to sleep!' Eventually my bedroom floors would calm down from the shaking they'd had. Such goings on here, I didn't know if this was odd, or as it should be – I was still learning.

Life settled down for a while, but then the noises at night started again. Ann lay in bed holding her breath, listening hard.

'It's definitely coming from above, but I can't make out if it's our attic or next door,' said Ann, talking to herself as usual. 'It seems to be in the walls too, I hope we've not got mice. But it doesn't sound like mice nor does it happen all the time.' Then quiet, nothing.

If only I was able to put her mind at rest!

The girls each left school in turn, worked in the same building. Started going out with friends to dances, cinemas and youth clubs; met and went out with boys, not always telling their parents. Hearing this was all new to me. I didn't understand any of it. Not as many arguments then, but when they happened there was lots of banging of bedroom doors, making me shake. After the first bang, I waited for the next one; there would always be a next one!

When Julie was 21, she planned to get married at St Saviour's Church, whatever that might mean. It seems I could see its spire above the other houses. So that's what it was! Beth was to be a bridesmaid; thrilled to wear a long dress of deep turquoise. On the morning of the wedding I heard Julie walking down the stairs quietly, dressed in her long white dress. She looked beautiful. I felt proud watching her, a grown woman now. Her dad was waiting at the bottom.

'Do you realise you have your slippers on?' he said. Both of them laughed as she dashed back up my stairs for her wedding shoes.

It was good being so happy, but I was also sad as I wasn't able to see what went on once they left.

Julie moved away after her wedding, and two years later, it was Beth's turn to marry and she too moved out. Both said goodbye to me, the only house they had ever known. They always felt so warm and loved here. I missed them both!

With Ann and John alone, it was quieter, but at least the girls were living not too far away and could visit regularly. It was fun when they did. They would chat away, filling my rooms with so much laughter and gaiety. This was a nice change for us!

That's when it started again, the noises, just like before. After a couple of nights of this, Ann was not sleeping well.

I heard her talking to herself. She was saying, 'I must tell John. This time I know I'm not dreaming,' while giving his shoulder a shake. 'John wake up!' Nothing but a grunt; another shake, this time he took notice.

'What's the matter, what's going on?' said John only half awake, and sitting up in bed rubbing his eyes and yawning.

'Just listen. Did you hear that? I've heard it before, but never said anything. What do you think it is?'

'Yes, I did hear something! Can it be from next door?'

'Not at this time John. Mrs Ball goes to bed early, and Sally and Dave are away on holiday this weekend.'

'It's gone quiet now, I can't hear a sound, I'll look into it in the morning. Now let's get some sleep.' He turned over and snuggled back under the covers.

Looks like it won't be long before they find out just what's going on!

The next day was Saturday. John's first job after breakfast was to get into my loft and investigate what, if anything, could be causing the noises from last night. Lifting my trap door and armed with a torch, John stood precariously on the step ladders which hardly reached the opening. With one elbow leaning against the edge he scanned the light around my loft space.

'Nothing! I can't see anything from here Ann. To see better I'll need a longer set of ladders. I'll borrow some from work.'

John brought a longer set of ladders home on Monday evening. 'These are much better Ann.'

He climbed through my opening with a larger torch to see if there was a problem. It was then he noticed that there was only a half wall between me and the adjoining houses. On the floorboards were biscuit wrappers and pop bottles.

'Looks like there's been someone up here. I think it must be children – looking at what they've left,' John shouted.

At last!

Over coffee, Ann and John shared their thoughts. 'I bet it's those two teenagers from next door but one: Mark and Phillip,' Ann said. 'They must have been coming through Mrs Ball's loft to ours when their parents went out at night. That's why I didn't hear the noises every night.'

'It's been going on over a number of years hasn't it?'

'Yes, but don't forget they have older brothers who have probably shown them the ropes. You can do something about it, can't you John?'

'I'll be bricking up the rest of the dividing walls, but before that I think we should catch them, give them a fright.'

Ann went to number eight and knocked on the door. I could just about hear, 'Hello Ann, come on in,' from Mrs Scott.

'Not just now thanks, but can you come to our house for a few minutes? John and I want to run something past you and Mr Scott.'

While the Scotts settled on the sofa, Ann went to brew tea as John explained just what had been happening over the years, and their plan. Mr and Mrs Scott were incensed; couldn't believe what their sons had been up to.

'Of course we'll go along with your plan John,' Mr Scott said.

I couldn't wait to see what happened next.

Next evening the plan was put into practice. John climbed up the ladders, sat in the far corner of my loft and quietly waited. Ann and the boy's parents sat below on the landing. Soon they could hear a slight noise, muffled sounds and see a faint light flashing in the dark. Next, loud screams when John stepped out of the shadows. The boys took flight, scrambled back the way they'd come to reach home and safety, or so they thought.

'We'll go back now and have more than a few harsh words with them,' Mr Scott said as they made for home.

'I think you really gave them a fright, John,' Ann said, grinning from ear to ear. 'What a night!'

Thank goodness this has all come to light at last. I'd wanted to tell Ann for years, but there was no way I could explain!

Things calmed down at number four with Ann, John and me jogging along merrily together, until one Saturday morning. Ann came dashing back from shopping, gasping for breath.

'Things are going to change for Parliament Street and the streets either side. I've heard rumours in the shop,' Ann told John. 'It seems the council intend to pull the houses down and the church. New houses and a supermarket are to be built on the land.'

I didn't know what that would mean to me!

'Don't panic yet Ann, it may not be true,' John said putting his arm around her.

A week later, Mrs Ball, Ann and Sally came together to discuss what if anything they could do. Ann accepted the inevitable.

'The trouble is there's nothing we can do. Once the council have decided, that's usually it! We've received our compulsory purchase orders, and now know the rumours are true. I don't want to move, neither does John.'

'We've all lived here happily together for years. I thought I'd end my days in my little house, in this street, with friends around,' Mrs Ball sobbed.

Sally didn't want to move either. 'Dave and I have had our ups and downs in our house I know, but everything has turned out great. We get along well these days. I hope moving won't alter things.'

What did it all mean? Moving, pulling the houses down? I didn't understand – what houses?

Months went by. The street outside stayed the same, but then I noticed a change. It was starting to get busy out there; much more than usual. People coming and going, all sorts of vans and other vehicles going past my window. Ann and John, with their friends, started taking their furniture away. What was going on?

*

Everyone has moved out. The other houses stand empty, as am I. The street is quiet there's no one here now. Why have things changed? What's happening? Where are Ann and John? I'm all alone again!

There are strange noises that are getting louder and louder, and getting nearer and nearer. The loud noise makes the ground shake and then I start to shudder. Now it's next to me; almost on top of me. Then, I feel it!

My front wall collapses. My lovely blue front door with its oval window lies there in the street, broken and smashed. I begin to feel my roof fall in, then, brick by brick I start to fall apart. With each brick that falls I lose a little of Lily, the twins, Julie and Beth, and all who have lived here.

Soon … I will not remember.

The Dalnessie Assignment

By Kerrie McKinnel

Behind closed doors.

Hidden.

Rose sat at the bay window, her cheek pressed to the cold glass, and watched the outside world tick along like the workings of her grandfather clock. Nine-thirty: the postman. No one else would go past now until the next morning. Beyond the road, Avoch Bay stretched out like a mirror beneath the cyan sky and overhanging trees. She could look at that view all day. Most days, she did nothing else.

Twenty years ago, when Rose and Arthur first viewed the house, it was the view from the living room which clinched it. The landlord hovered behind them as they paused to survey the shimmering water.

'Oh Artie,' she squealed. 'Look. Isn't that beautiful? This is it. This is the house.'

'You can get a view like that over the Firth of Forth.'

'Artie, you're terrible!' She giggled and kissed him. 'That isn't the point and you know it. Where in Edinburgh does it smell this fresh? And the peace and quiet! It's incredible.' She stepped towards the window and pressed a palm to the glass. 'In the city, everybody knows your business. You could do what you liked here and nobody would ever know.'

'It's over our budget, Rosie Cheeks. I'd have to work overtime for the rest of my life to pay the rent on this.'

'Please? I can just picture it, can't you? The children skipping down to the—'

'Children? We've only been married a month! I'm already moving to the other end of the country so you can indulge your little Highland fantasy. Can't you be content with that?'

The landlord's snort of laughter soured Arthur's mood, but it wasn't long before Rose's enthusiasm had him convinced. In the summer of 1931, they packed up their one-bedroom flat and moved their lives 166 miles north to Dalnessie House.

In those newly-wed days, tradesmen streamed into the house like sunshine. Weekends were spent wandering Inverness hand in hand to choose just the right painting for the wall above the mantlepiece. Rose remembered barefoot dashes across the lawn and into the water, hazy summer air filled with joyous screams and Arthur's shouts of, 'Come on in, Rosie, and feel the temperature of the water! That'll put some colour into your cheeks!'; hot kisses on cold skin, whiskies by the log fire, late nights at the bay window daydreaming of the bedrooms which they would one day fill with children's laughter.

When the Second World War dawned, crisp and real and all too soon, Rose found herself alone with only her daydreams. *Come home safely, my hero,* she wrote, *love from your Rosie Cheeks.* The Army gave him leave but, as he explained in his brief replies, not long enough for him to return all the way to their Highland home. *But why?* she longed to ask, knowing that the women in the nearby village had received visits from their husbands. But her heart told her not to doubt him.

Each day she watched Avoch Bay shift under the ever-changing clouds, while she sat at the bay window and wrote: letters to her beloved, journal entries, wherever she found a space on a piece of paper, as if writing his name over and over would guarantee his safe return.

And then one day there he was. It was a miserable evening and she was so mesmerised by the rain running down the outside of the glass that she didn't recognise him at first, the tall muscular figure in the dark greatcoat and hat, until he drew closer to the house. She ran outside and threw her arms around him.

'Artie!' The rain ran into her eyes, soaking through her dressing gown and slippers, but she didn't care. *His lips were like kissing stone, but he would be tired after his journey,* she thought, *just desperate to get home.* 'Artie, darling, I'm so glad to see you.'

'What are you trying to do – freeze me to death? Move yourself, woman,' he growled, and pushed her aside.

Perplexed, she pulled the front door shut against the night. He was drenched and exhausted, of course. She slid her sodden slippers off onto the hallway floor and waited behind him.

'Look at the place – the filth on this dresser. And the cobwebs, Rose.' Arthur surveyed the hallway while he unbuttoned his greatcoat.

'Are you tired, darling?' she asked as she edged forwards to take his coat. 'A whisky? Something to eat? There's homemade jam and bread, or something more? I could—'

'Move out of the *way!* Dear God woman, can't I have a few minutes peace in my own home before you start badgering me with questions? The women on the continent were less trouble.'

Rose felt as if the bottom had fallen out of her stomach. 'Women?'

'You didn't expect me to wait six years, did you? What else was I meant to do while I was on leave?' Arthur took out a cigarette and lit it. Smoke swirled in front of Rose's face.

'But you … why didn't you come back here when you were on leave, like the other men?'

'And waste half my time off trailing all the way back to this dump?'

Rose's heart hesitated as she struggled for words. The only sound was the drip-drip-drip as brown water pooled beneath the greatcoat, which she clutched to her stomach.

'But … but Artie.'

The next night, he raised a fist to her.

At church a couple of months later, directly after the Sunday morning service, she finally found the courage and opportunity to speak privately to the minister.

'Shell shock,' he nodded, and patted her arm. 'With time …'

'But I've given him time,' Rose whispered, glancing over her shoulder in case Arthur should finish his conversation with the local butcher. 'You don't understand. I—'

The minister held up his hand. 'It is between yourselves and God. Now, have you been saying your daily prayers? And do you take care to cook him a hearty dinner each night?'

There was a time when she'd found it impossible to think of the old Artie without crying, but the subsequent days, months and years – beatings, cigarette ends and the threats of a blow from the cricket bat in the hallway cupboard – deadened her. Terror left no room for emotion. He began to go out more, often without warning, and sometimes for a day or two at a time.

'Is a man not allowed to go fishing by himself anymore?' he snapped whenever she asked where he'd been. She knew better than to press him, despite the smell of perfume which lingered on his greatcoat.

The bells had not long rung for the new year, 1951, when Arthur disappeared for good. In his wake, he left nothing except relief and a quiet, deep-seated dread of the day that he might reappear.

Now, Rose gazed out at the view of Avoch Bay that had sustained her through the last six months of solitude. Money grew tighter every day; surely her dwindling rent payments would be noticed soon, but at least for the moment she felt safe within the walls of Dalnessie House. If she ever had to leave, how would she survive?

*

Summer in Scotland: Hector Scott should have known better than to depend on it. As he drove onto the ferry from Inverness, he saw the first spits of rain on the windscreen. Turning up the collar of his soot-black coat against the gathering winds, he made his way to the passenger cabin. *An umbrella would have been more useful than a fedora*, he thought, *but at least the greatcoat offers some warmth.*

Hector had planned to get through some paperwork on the journey, but all he could think about now was a cigarette. He rested his shoulder against the glass pane and waited for the judder as the Kessock ferry pulled away and began its journey north towards the Black Isle.

'Isn't this fabulous?' the woman behind remarked to her friend. 'To think, a ferry just for cars and people! The times I've spent on that old boat with the farm animals.'

Hector smiled to himself. The route was so familiar to him now that he rarely thought about it. It was possible to drive to the Black Isle by travelling inland, but the twisting rural roads made for a long and difficult journey. As a reporter for Highland Homes Magazine, he'd spent the years since World War Two travelling the north of Scotland in search of his next featured property. Travel exhausted him; his leg still ached from a gunshot wound sustained six years earlier, in the last days of the war. He longed for a nine-to-five desk job, but recent troubles at the magazine and approaching retirement meant he had little option but to accept whatever work came his way.

'The magazine is in trouble,' the editor had told them a few months earlier. 'Everyone has to work harder for their pay cheque. There will be no dead weight.'

The week after this announcement, one of Hector's colleagues was fired.

There will be no dead weight.

Hector flicked through the details of his assignment. Dalnessie House was well known in architectural circles: a fine Georgian house dating from the early to mid-1700s, constructed around the same time as the first Fort George. There were no known photographs of the house's interior. *Landlord has written to tenants informing them of your arrival,* he read from his notes. The landlord, according to his editor, was only interested in the fee; maintaining a property of this age was not cheap.

The house was less than 30 minutes from the harbour; Hector would be done in time to catch the last sailing of the night. He pulled his collar further up, lit another cigarette, and steeled himself for the day ahead.

By the time the ferry reached Kessock, the rain had become heavier. It fell from the heavens in sheets, drenching the green countryside and overwhelming the car's windscreen wipers. After stopping twice to ask for directions, Hector finally pulled up outside the property. The needle on the dashboard told him that he had just enough fuel to get back to the harbour to catch the return ferry.

Dalnessie House sat behind a gravelled turning circle and ten-foot-high fountain. Manicured grounds sprawled out towards the west, as far as could be seen through the rain. Beyond, the waters stretched out into the gloom. He shivered.

'Come on,' Hector said out loud, bracing himself. 'The sooner you get this damned job done, the sooner you can get back on the road.'

He tucked his notes into his pocket, jumped out and sprinted to the front door. A narrow porch offered no protection from the rain, which seemed to blow in every direction. He stood hunched inside his coat as he rang the doorbell twice, thrice, four times. He tried the handle: locked. Taking out his flashlight, he squelched to the nearest window to check for signs of life. Even through the wet glass, his mood lifted a little to see the ornate plaster ceilings, full-height windows, and antique furnishings waiting for him inside. Exquisite paintings adorned the walls: family portraits, he assumed. He could already imagine a four-page … no, six-page article in the magazine. He would be the talk of the magazine. His job would be secure, for another few months at least.

There would be nothing, however, if he couldn't get into the house. He tried the doorbell once more: no answer. After a fruitless circuit of the house, there was nothing left to do except return to his car and wait. Perhaps the tenants had been delayed. They would return soon, no doubt.

Minutes turned into hours. He watched the hands tick round on his watch while he cursed, thumped the steering wheel, and smoked his last cigarette. If he didn't leave now, he'd miss the last ferry, but what choice did he have?

There will be no dead weight.

He had to get the story.

Hector pinched the skin between his eyebrows in a vain attempt to distract his brain from his growing anger. *Calm down,* he reprimanded himself. A misunderstanding, surely. Crossed wires. When the tenants returned, he would be ready to hear their apologies and then get on with the job. Hector reclined his seat, stretched out his aching leg, and switched on the car radio. With his greatcoat in lieu of a blanket, it was fairly comfortable.

Rain drummed on the car roof. Hector's thoughts trailed back over his journey. There had been a town a few minutes' drive away. There might be a bed and breakfast. It would cost him more than he would end up being paid for the assignment, but he could return in the morning, washed and fed, and try once more before he left. There would be just enough fuel for that … he hoped. Perhaps someone in the town could give directions to a petrol station. His stomach rumbled, his neck crunched with tension, and he had smoked his last cigarette. If he was going to keep his job, he needed to be in a fit state to wait around for the story. It was the best solution in a woeful situation.

He turned the key and his heart sank as the engine tried but failed to burst into life. Twice more he tried, and twice more the car shuddered and died. Of course: the radio had run down the battery. His head slumped forwards onto the steering wheel and he let out a moan. Now this, on top of everything else; he simply could not face a full night in his car.

He was glancing around in the darkness, trying to think of another option, when he saw a light from the house. It came from upstairs, brief and faint but unmistakable. His aching body sprang back to life. He wiped the condensation from the window. Had someone sneaked past him into the house? Impossible. He'd been waiting for hours. Whoever it was had been there all the time. Asleep, perhaps, and hadn't heard him? No, he'd hammered on the front door, shouted, and knocked on most of the windows. They'd deliberately ignored him.

The light reappeared downstairs in the hallway. It flickered like a candle in the darkness. It approached the front door, paused, and then disappeared.

They'd seen him.

They didn't want to be seen.

Hector's feet thumped on the floor of the car, his hands now trembling with rage. Whoever was inside didn't care that he'd waited in sodden clothes for several hours, or that this miserable assignment was about to cost him his job. His icy skin prickled as he grabbed his fedora and jumped out of the car. This time he barely noticed the rain which beat down on him as he sprinted to the door.

'Open up!' he yelled. The wooden door rattled under the force of his fists. 'Open up. I know you're in there.'

No response.

Had he imagined it? Perhaps it had been a reflection … but no! The candle reappeared at what he took to be the far end of the hallway, just for a moment but long enough for him to be sure. They were hiding – the cowards! An inhuman roar erupted from deep within him.

'Open this door!' he bellowed. 'This is Hector Scott from Highland Homes Magazine. I know you can hear me.'

The candle wavered and then drew closer. Hector attempted to steady himself and his breathing. It was unprofessional to lose his temper in front of a client. *Come on Hector, final effort.* Click, clunk, thud: he heard keys being turned, locks undone. And then the door opened, ever so slightly.

'Mr Scott, did you say?'

The voice had a high-class Edinburgh accent, female, soft. Through the gap Hector saw a sliver of blonde hair and pale skin. He strained to hear her over the rain.

'I am sorry Mr Scott, but I do not receive visitors. Goodbye.'

She made to close the door, but he pushed against it.

'Madam, I have been waiting for you all afternoon – all evening, in fact,' Hector said, his voice strained. Another deep breath, in and out. She wouldn't let him in if she thought he was violent. 'Mrs Connolly, isn't it? Your landlord wrote to you? You should be expecting me. I just need to take a few photographs and then—'

'No, most certainly not. No, no, I'm sorry but you must leave.'

'I don't think you're listening, Mrs Connolly.' He grimaced as his body shook with cold and pent-up rage. 'You don't understand what you're asking me to do. If I go back to the office without this story, I'll lose my job.'

'Go away now. Or I shall call the police.' She made to close the door again; Hector jammed his shoe into the gap.

'Mr Scott,' she cried, panic underlying her Edinburgh accent. 'Remove your foot.'

'No, I will not!' Hector rammed his arm onto the wet wood of the door. She held the door more firmly than he'd expected, but gradually he felt it give way. 'Let – me – in!' he yelled, louder with each push. 'I will not leave without my story.'

'Stop it Artie, stop it!'

Artie? he wondered, but he was too swept up in anger to think about it. 'You would have me lose my job over this!' he yelled. 'My life! My livelihood!'

'Arthur, please!' Her voice had become a scream. 'Go away, or I shall do something which I'll regret.'

'I will not leave without my story. *I will not become dead weight!*'

The door flew open. It hit against the hallway wall. The bang echoed into the darkness.

Hector staggered into the house a couple of steps before he regained his balance.

'Mrs Connolly?'

He glanced around and narrowed his eyes in an attempt to make out a shape, but the wind had extinguished the candle. His stomach lurched as he looked down to the floor – could he have pushed her over or, worse, knocked her unconscious? What would his editor say to that?

'Mrs Connolly?' One of his hands found the wall. He knelt and patted the floor with the other hand, shuffling along as best he could in his crouched position, until he was satisfied that she hadn't fallen. But then, where was she?

'I didn't mean to scare you,' he called. *The poor woman must be terrified to feel the need to hide from me in this gloom,* he thought as he edged forwards, guided by the wall. 'Please, show yourself. I'm sorry. I won't hurt you. My car battery's died. Point me in the direction of the nearest garage, and I'll leave you in peace.'

Squinting into the shadows of the hallway, he fancied that he saw movement. Perhaps she had been standing there silently the whole time, waiting to see what he would do.

'Are you alright, Mrs Connolly? I'm sorry, I—'

A scream pierced him from behind.

'No, Arthur! You won't hurt me again.'

Before Hector could turn towards the voice, there was a sharp pain in the back of his head and the sensation of falling into nothingness.

*

The next day dawned bright and clear. Rose woke early and settled at the bay window for her usual cup of tea, but this morning she couldn't stop her fingers from trembling.

And then, finally, nine-thirty: the postman. No one else would go past now until the next morning.

Rose stood, set down her empty cup, and slipped on a cardigan. It felt strange to turn the locks in the front door; it creaked as she eased it open and stepped outside. On the path, she paused to gaze up at the cyan sky. The breeze felt strange and beautiful on her skin. She drew in a deep breath of summer air and let it out slowly. It was just as she'd remembered.

Rose ambled towards Avoch Bay. The waters stretched out in front of her, still and silent. It felt like a lifetime since those newly-wed days when they would sit here together, Artie murmuring into her ear, 'I've done well to end up with you, Rosie Cheeks.'

Where had that man gone? What was shell shock? Why had it affected him the way it did? There were so many things that she now feared she might never understand. The man who had returned from the war: he was the real shell. A body without a heart.

There were times when he became so violent that she feared for her life, and other times when misery overwhelmed her and she wished he *would* kill her.

Hard, then, to feel guilty about how things had ended.

She slipped off her shoes, sat down by the water's edge and dipped her toes into the cool water. She hadn't left the house since that January day six months ago when Arthur had disappeared. Now, with the sun on her cheeks, she wondered why she'd left it so long to return to her favourite spot. Perhaps one day she would venture into town and see if she could have a bench erected here in Artie's memory – the real Artie, the one she'd married. It was such a peaceful place to reflect.

Still, the sun was creeping higher in the sky, and she had work to do. Getting to her feet, she was overwhelmed for a moment by a strange sense of déjà vu – memories of the wheelbarrow's wheels crunching over ice – but she quickly dismissed them and concentrated on her morning's task. It took all of her strength to push the barrow across the stones and far enough out into the water, but once it was empty the return trip was easier.

Her work done, Rose sat back down on the grass to dry her feet and replace her shoes. The breeze ruffled the tips of her long blonde hair and played with the hem of her dress. She smiled. This really had been a pleasant morning.

About Lockerbie Writers

By Kerrie McKinnel

Lockerbie Writers are a like-minded group of local writers. The group share work and provide supportive critique and motivation as they improve their understanding of the craft of creative writing. An active group of approximately ten members, Lockerbie Writers meet fortnightly on a Tuesday in Lockerbie, south-west Scotland. Throughout the year, they produce writing inspired by a range of prompts.

Alongside their own writing, another of the group's interests is inspiring writing in others. In 2017, they established an annual children's writing competition in collaboration with Castle Loch Community Trust (Lochmaben); this competition now runs annually. They also run regular writing workshops, events and members' days.

Lockerbie Writers published their first collection of work, *Lockerbie Writers' Anthology: Stories and Poems from Annandale and Eskdale,* in spring 2016. It was initially developed as part of my own university project. The book is a collection of short stories and poetry in a range of genres, reflecting the diversity of the group. The publication received excellent feedback from the local community and beyond, and is available to buy from Amazon.co.uk or directly from the group.

In 2017, spurred on by the success of their first anthology, the group began to talk about producing a second volume – but this time, without the pressing deadlines of a university assignment, they agreed to take it more slowly. Over the next two years, members went through a time-consuming and substantial editing and peer review process, before arriving at the finished product which you hold in your hands today.

It is with a huge amount of pride, therefore, that I end this anthology by thanking you for reading the results of our hard work.

For more information about Lockerbie Writers or their sister group, A Novel Approach, please visit www.lockerbiewritersanthology.wordpress.com **or search on Facebook for 'Lockerbie Writers'.**

Biographies

Betsy Henderson is married with two grown-up children and three grandchildren. She has always liked writing and since her retirement she has made it one of her hobbies. She particularly enjoys the prompts from Lockerbie Writers which take her more and more out of her comfort zone. Another of her passions is learning about local history, and especially her own family history.

Chris Openshaw, after finishing work in 2013, joined Lockerbie Writers. Her inspiration comes from her background in Lancashire and latterly from the countryside in which she lives. She has never missed a Lockerbie Writers' prompt, and enjoys working to them and seeing where they take her.

Deborah Redden, a Lockerbie Writers' member based in Ireland, is the proud mother of two young boys who inspire her every day. For her, a day without writing/sketching is a rare commodity – ten minutes can always be snatched from somewhere. She has been interested in writing and illustration for as long as she can remember, and attributes a sizeable chunk of her passion in this area to the magical marriage that is Roald Dahl and Quentin Blake.

Frank MacGregor is a retired businessman and lives with his wife Marjorie in Lockerbie. He is a member of Lockerbie Writers and A Novel Approach. He has always had a lively interest in history and is currently in the final throes of writing a novel centred around the seventeenth century Scottish civil wars.

Godfrey Newham is a publishing editor, keen reader, music lover and hill-walker. He has lived in Annan since 2013. He believes that good editing is the key to presenting good writing, and hopes that this anthology will encourage readers to share his belief.

Kath J. Rennie: After a visit to Lockerbie in 1984, Kath decided to move to the town with her family. She finds rural life more in keeping with her love of nature, which has inspired many pieces of published poetry. In 2015, Kath joined Lockerbie Writers group, where she was inspired to write short stories and continues to do so … She is a mother of three sons, a step-son and five granddaughters.

Kerrie McKinnel is Lockerbie Writers' Events Manager and a founding member of A Novel Approach. Her writing has been featured in publications including *Gutter, Southlight* and *From Glasgow to Saturn.* She lives with her husband and two young children, who inspire much of her writing. Since completing her MLitt Creative Writing (University of Glasgow), Kerrie has run a number of successful writing workshops and events, and compiled and co-edited Lockerbie Writers' first and second anthologies. Kerrie also runs writing workshops and events for all ages through her business, Kerrie McKinnel – Writer. For more information visit: www.kerriemckinnel.com

Paula Nicolson is PR Manager for Lockerbie Writers and a member of A Novel Approach. Paula lives near Lockerbie with her family and the ashes of her dead cat. She enjoys laughing, writing and eating cake; preferably all at the same time. Paula also writes a blog on life in Dumfries and Galloway which can be found at: www.facebook.com/deckywriting

Rita Dalgliesh is a member of Lockerbie Writers, and has never missed a prompt. She enjoys stretching her imagination through her writing. Rita also loves reading, in particular historical war novels. She recently joined a book group in Annan, which has encouraged her to try a wide range of genres and given her an insight into a whole new world of authors.

Steph Newham is Lockerbie Writers' chairperson. She retired from the NHS where she had used storytelling as a therapeutic tool. On retirement she did a Cert in Creative Writing followed by an MA at Lancaster University. She is currently working on a collection of short stories as well as a historical novel. She has had articles published in newspapers and non-fiction journals. Her short stories are published in several anthologies and online e-zines. She enjoys running workshops and encouraging others to develop their writing skills.

Vivien Jones writes short stories, poetry and pieces for performance. She leads projects for aspiring writers, especially working with museums and galleries to bring artefacts to life on the page. She is one of three editors of *Southlight*, the region's literature magazine, and is a Literature Ambassador for Wigtown Book Festival.

Members of Lockerbie Writers on their summer outing to Lochmaben Castle, July 2019. The group were entertained and inspired by ghost stories from local paranormal investigation team Mostly Ghostly, before visiting Lochfield Cottage (Castle Loch Community Trust) to write. Many of the resulting stories were published on their blog during Halloween 2019 and can be viewed at:

https://lockerbiewritersanthology.wordpress.com

Pictured (left to right): Rita Dalgliesh, Frank MacGregor, Betsy Henderson, Kerrie McKinnel, Paula Nicolson, Laura Mason, Christina Openshaw, Kath J. Rennie and Richard Sharp.

A Lockerbie Writers' meeting at the Townhead Hotel, Lockerbie, in April 2019.

Pictured (clockwise around the table from bottom left): Christina Openshaw, Frank MacGregor, Paula Nicolson, Godfrey Newham, Steph Newham, Richard Sharp, Kerrie McKinnel, Kath J. Rennie, Rita Dalgliesh and Betsy Henderson.

Lockerbie Writers' member Deborah Redden, who lives in Ireland and is an active online group member, visited the group in person during summer 2019. She is pictured here with Chairperson Steph Newham.

In June 2019, Lockerbie Writers hosted their first mindful writing day. Thanks to the support of DG Unlimited and Dumfries and Galloway Council, they were able to invite published writer Margaret Elphinstone to speak and tutor at the event. The day was attended by almost thirty people and was a huge success.

Pictured: Rita Dalgliesh, Paula Nicolson, Steph Newham, Kerrie McKinnel and Kath J. Rennie.

Lockerbie Writers

Write - Critique - Support

If you have enjoyed reading this book, please leave us a review on Amazon.co.uk – and don't forget to spread the word!

Thank you.

Lockerbie Writers

November 2019

Printed in Poland
by Amazon Fulfillment
Poland Sp. z o.o., Wrocław

50279876R00079